DOG

DOG

ANDY MULLIGAN

PUSHKIN CHILDREN'S

Pushkin Press
71–75 Shelton Street
London, WC2H 9JQ

First published by Pushkin Press in 2017

1 3 5 7 9 8 6 4 2

ISBN 978 1 782691 71 6

Designed and typeset by M Rules, London
Printed and bound by
CPI Group (UK) Ltd, Croydon CR0 4YY

www.pushkinpress.com

For Joe

PART ONE

The dog had no name.

He'd been alive for just eleven and a half weeks, and every day had been bewildering. Five brothers had disappeared, along with two sisters: they'd simply left, without a bark of goodbye— and they hadn't come back. His mother was nearby, but in a different part of the house. He could hear her sometimes when the door opened, but she didn't come to see him. That made him lonely. He was in a cardboard box, and the only creature he occasionally saw was a long, silver cat that perched outside on the window sill, with her nose against the glass. She stared at him without blinking, and when he tried to get her attention she simply turned her back.

He lay on his side and studied his paws. There were four altogether, and they were black and white. So was the rest of him: a pattern of swirls and splodges ran right around his body and up to his ears, which flopped over his face. He flicked them aside, and played with his tail. Tired of that, he rolled on to his back, squirming on the blanket beneath him.

Was he hungry? No. There were things to chew, and he'd just had a drink. He was warm enough, too, and he'd spent part of the morning happily scratching. The problem was boredom, for without siblings there was nobody to nip, lick or nuzzle.

There was nobody to talk to, so when he noticed the spider, he sat bolt upright, and kept absolutely still. It was dangling from the lampshade over his head, and he watched hopefully as it descended. Soon, it was hovering just above his nose. The dog twitched, determined not to snap, and the creature rotated carefully. A moment later, it had landed right between his eyes, where it divided into two and grew blurred. Sixteen legs flexed and stretched, while innumerable eyes gazed with a solemn seriousness that was quite terrifying.

It was clearly a time for courage.

"Hello?" said the dog nervously. "Good morning."

The spiders said nothing. They moved back slowly, and coalesced into a single black dot. A pair of fangs appeared, and the eyes grew brighter.

"Good morning," it said. "How are you?"

"I'm well, thank you. And I'm certainly glad to see you, because I was wondering if I'd be alone again all day. Everyone's left me, so I was getting quite... well, worried."

"Rightly so," said the spider. Its mouth stretched into a tiny smile.

"Do you know where they've gone?"

4

"I do not."

"So what's happening?"

"Nothing. You're curious, though—which doesn't surprise me. You want the truth, of course—you want answers that will help you assess the situation and decide on an appropriate strategy. But before I give them to you, friend, I'd better warn you about something. Spiders never lie, because it's not in their nature: we can only deal with facts."

"Then that's perfect," said the dog. "I'm feeling quite confused, you see. I don't want to be impatient, but I'm not sure how much longer I can stand this."

"Your family's been sold," said the spider. "It happened fast."

"And who have they been sold to?"

"Different people. Money changed hands, and they're all on their way to happy new homes, where they're going to be loved and looked after. They'll be settling in even as we speak, getting to know nice families. That's the joy of being wanted, you see. The problem for you is that you were rejected. You're the one nobody chose."

"Oh. Right."

The dog sat in silence, and the spider moved up on to his forehead. It went higher, resting between his ears, before picking one of them. It squeezed under the flap, and spoke softly.

"Can you hear me?"

"Yes."

"You're the youngest and the smallest. Take a look at yourself, little dog: you're weak, and you're skinny. OK, you might put on weight in due course, but you're still lopsided and clumsy. You're out of proportion, too, and you're probably not aware of it, but when you close your mouth, your jaws don't shut properly. One tooth remains visible, so you look awkward. Your brothers were more attractive, I'm afraid—as were your sisters. That's the law of this particular jungle: the strong survive, and the weak go under. Do you have any more questions at this stage?"

"I don't think so. No."

"Think hard."

The dog blinked again. "I suppose I do have one," he said nervously. "If I haven't been chosen, then... OK. It means I'm not wanted at the moment, and I understand that—"

"Those are the facts, and you have to face them."

"Yes. But what's going to happen to me? I can't stay here, can I?"

"No. So you've been given away. Do you remember the man who visited this morning? He picked you up and inspected you."

"Yes. He was in a hurry."

"He certainly was, but I took the liberty of climbing on to his jacket, and I heard everything he said. He was looking for a pet, and he'd hoped to get a kitten. He popped in here because of the sign on the door: 'One puppy left, free to a good home.' That's what it said, so in he came in search of a bargain. He decided to give you a try, apparently. You're going to be a gift to his son."

"But he didn't take me. He's left me."

"He's coming back, or sending someone. You'll be on your way very soon."

The dog shook himself with excitement.

"So that means I *am* wanted," he yelped. "I *have* been chosen."

"I wouldn't say that. I wouldn't jump to that conclusion, little dog, and I wouldn't get my hopes up. It's not a good start, after all. The family lives in a small house, for one thing—and they don't have much money. The boy is called Tom, and he's just started at some fancy new school, so—reading between the lines—I think you might be a reward of some kind, like a trophy, or a prize. There have been a few changes in the household, by the sound of it. A bit of upheaval. So the ideal pet, logically, was a safe, straightforward cat. You've been purchased on a whim: you're an experiment."

"Wow," said the dog. "I'd better be good, then. I'll need to be *better* than a cat, and make sure I don't cause any problems."

"Is that possible?"

"Yes! Of course it is."

The dog shook himself again, more anxious than ever. The spider moved back to his nose, and its smile was wide.

"Dear, oh dear," it said, chuckling. "What does the future hold, I wonder? You don't have a pedigree, so nobody knows what's in the mix. Are you a hunter, perhaps? I doubt it. Are you a guard dog? No. Are you decorative, or functional? Loving, loyal—?"

"I could be all those things!"

"Or none of them."

"I'm friendly, at least."

"You're a fool, and you're unlucky."

The dog winced. His head was aching slightly, and he was seeing double again.

"What's the boy's name? I think you told me, but—"

"Tom."

"I like that. It's a nice name, and it's easy to say. I wonder what he'll call me?"

"If it gets that far. If you don't get rejected in the first five minutes."

"I need a name!"

"Are names so important?"

"Yes! Very."

"Why?"

"I don't know. Without a name you're... nothing. What's yours?"

"I've never had one, my friend. I'm nameless, but I still exist."

"Can I call you Thread?" said the dog. "Would you answer to that?"

The spider laughed. It kicked itself into the air, and wound itself upwards, twirling happily.

"Call me what you like," it cried. "We may never meet again..."

The dog watched as it disappeared, but even as he yelped his goodbye the door was opening. There stood the woman who'd been feeding him. She picked him up, and, before he could even twist, he was in the hall, where a young man was waiting with a leather bag. The dog allowed himself to be lowered into it, trembling all over. It was happening, just as the spider had predicted.

The woman stroked his head and tickled his chin.

"Have a good life, angel," she said. "You only get one."

8

2

Tom was in the back garden.

The flower beds were thick with weeds, and the grass hadn't been cut for several weeks. The whole area was turning into a wilderness, in fact. Tom sat surrounded by sockets and spanners. An old engine lay in pieces around him: the components were on newspaper, ready to be cleaned.

The back door opened, and he saw his father.

"You're needed," he said.

"Who by?"

"There's something for you. Can you wipe your hands? It's a special delivery, I think—just arrived."

Tom stood up. There was a rag to the side, so he cleaned his fingers. He could see Phil in the kitchen, and he still had his helmet on. As he came closer to the window he saw a bag on the table, and he noticed that his father's face was expressionless.

"What's going on?"

"Nothing."

"What have you got for me? What's in there?"

His dad had moved back inside, so Tom followed.

"I don't know," he said. "It was on the doorstep. I was going to send it back, but then I saw it had your name on it."

"If it's from Mum, I'm not opening it."

"I don't think it is."

"Where's it come from, then?"

"I don't know. What is it, Phil? You carried it in."

"No idea. It's heavy, though, and there's something moving about."

Tom stood in the doorway, and felt his stomach contract.

Phil had taken his helmet off now, and was looking at him with a curious smile.

His dad had moved to the cooker, and his face was still blank.

The radio was off, and the only sound was a sudden scratching from inside the bag, which caused it to expand and contract. The zip was fastened, and Tom heard a soft, plaintive whine.

"What is it?" he asked.

"Maybe it's a football," said Phil.

"It's something for school, I expect," said his dad. "A nice new blazer."

"I've got one already."

"A spare?"

Tom found that he couldn't breathe. He shook his head, and

for a moment he thought he was going to choke. Swallowing, he realized that something funny had happened to his hands: they were clasped together, just under his nose, and for some reason he had tears in his eyes.

"You haven't..." he said quietly. "Have you?"

"Haven't what?"

"I'd given up asking. Dad, you haven't..."

"What's he talking about, Phil?"

"I've no idea. He's looking a bit shaky, though. Are you ill, Tom? Do you want to lie down?"

"I think we'd better get help—he's gone all pink."

Tom walked to the table. The bag had moved again: he had seen it jump, and whatever was inside was very definitely alive. He wiped the tears from his eyes, but his fingers wouldn't work properly—he couldn't get the zip open, and he was aware that Phil had started filming it all on his phone. The thing inside was now whining continuously, and he distinctly heard a yap. At last, he got the zip to work. Even as it split open, a pair of paws pushed their way out, followed by a furry head. There was a tangle of ears, which separated to reveal shining eyes and then a nose that rose to meet Tom's with a howl of delight.

The dog launched itself upwards like a spring, twisting in mid-air. How had it been confined in so small a space? It exploded upwards and outwards, and Tom just managed to catch it under the forelegs and lift it clear, even as it squirmed round into his arms and licked his face.

The boy staggered backwards with the dog pressed against his chest.

"No way!" he said. "This can't be real..."

Phil was laughing, and so was his father.

11

Tom clutched the dog to himself, open-mouthed.

"I don't believe it!" he cried. "I absolutely don't believe it! Is this really for me?"

His father was nodding.

"But you said we couldn't... I don't believe it! No!"

"He's yours, Tom. Hard work pays off, and he really is yours."

"He can't be..."

"Yours for ever. So come on, put him down."

"I don't believe this... Look at him. Oh, just look at him!"

Tom sank to his knees, and let his dog down on to the kitchen floor. There was a scrabble of claws and a quick somersault of fur as the dog launched himself upwards again. He leapt under the table and over to Phil, and then seemed to bounce off the wall towards Tom, who scooped him up again as the dog clambered on to his shoulder.

"I'm dreaming!" cried Tom. "You said a cat, if I was lucky. You said a cat, maybe, and look at this!"

"You don't want him?"

"Oh, I do! He's... incredible. What shall I call him, though? He's got to have a name! Can I call him what I want?"

"Of course," said his dad. "Now put him down a second."

"Thank you, Dad. He's the most beautiful thing in the world. Just look at his legs—he's like a great big spider. *That's* what I'm going to call him! That's his name, all right? Oh, wow—this is the best day of my life..."

"It's only what I said, Tom—listen. You worked for that scholarship, and what with everything that's happened—"

"Oh, he's gorgeous..."

"You'll train him, and look after him. You're going to be responsible for him, OK? In every way."

The dog twisted again, and Tom held him tight against his ribcage. He could feel a heart beating, fast and furious.

"Look at his coat," he said softly. "Is he a sheepdog, do you think?"

Phil laughed. "I don't think he's that. He's got a bit of terrier in him, maybe."

"A bit of hyena," said his dad. "I can see crocodile, too—look at that tooth."

Tom didn't hear them.

"He's so stretchy," he cried. "Look at his tail, and his legs— they're tangled up. It's like he's got too many!"

His eyes were still running with tears, and the dog felt one bounce off his nose. He squirmed, and managed to get a good lick at the boy's face. He could smell Tom's hair because it was long and clean—there was soap mixed in with a cocktail of oil and garden. The boy was thin, and it occurred to the dog that in some ways they looked rather similar. Tom was grinning now, and his smile was absolutely joyful.

"I'm going to call him Spider," said Tom. "Is that OK?"

"Put him down, Tom. Let's get him a drink."

"Oh, Dad, thank you so much! Thank you, Phil—thank you. Come on, Spider—let's show you round, and get you some food."

"Be careful, mate," said Phil. "He's still only a puppy."

"I'll show him the house! This is your home now, Spider. This is where you live, so you better get to know it and guard it."

The boy put the dog gently down on to his four paws, and the dog was still for a moment. He stared around the room, taking in his new family and his surroundings. Within seconds, he'd bolted for the door and found himself in the open air, racing through the grass. Tom followed, shouting, so Spider swung round and instinctively dodged to the side, then he tore back the way he'd come. Moments later, he was jumping high, dashing between the boy's legs and turning tight circles. He snarled in ecstasy, play-biting and rolling on to his back.

"Spider!" cried Tom. "Come on, sir! Sit!"

The dog dived at his new master, barking madly.

"No, Spider! Down!"

Spider writhed again, and waved his legs in the air. He felt hands on his ribs, and right around his neck. Tom was wrestling him now, and as Spider fought he yelped in wonder. For a split second he thought of Thread, and yelped again, for the nasty little creature had got everything so totally, utterly wrong.

He had a home. He had a name. Best of all, he had an owner who needed him—and that was simply too good to be true.

Tom soon realized that Spider was a real explorer.

The dog loved the garden, which ended in a patch of mud and a mad mess of brambles. He'd glimpsed an alleyway that led towards some bins, and there was an empty shed beside a small, stagnant pond. The world was a shimmering cocktail of ever-changing smells, and Spider could lose himself among them for hours on end.

"We'll go further afield soon," said Tom, stroking his nose. "There's a park nearby, and you'll love it."

Spider blinked and licked Tom's fingers.

"You need proper exercise, don't you? I realize that. And we need to start serious training. Dad works nights, Spider, so there are times we have to be dead quiet. Oh, and you don't ever go into Phil's room. Phil's the guy who collected you. He's our lodger and he's a friend as well. He has a little pet, too, by the way. It's a fish, so his room's totally out of bounds. There are so many rules! It's just like school…"

Spider nibbled Tom's wrist, and dived up at his chin. They play-fought again, until Tom rolled on to his back and Spider lay on top of him, panting.

He had been waiting to meet the boy's brothers and sisters, but realized now that Tom was all on his own, and—like him—without a mother. Where the mother had gone was a mystery, for her scent was everywhere.

The lodger occupied the middle floor, and he was followed by a smell of engine oil and grease. Spider had glimpsed the fish, twirling in a bowl—and it didn't interest him. What interested him more than anything was his new master's bedroom, which was up another flight of stairs at the top of the house. It was a tent-like triangle, high in the roof space, where fresh air circulated all the time because of a skylight that wouldn't close. There were no curtains, so you could see the clouds by day and the stars by night. The carpet was covered in toys and clothes, so the first thing the dog had done was build a nest right in the middle of Tom's bed, using both pillows and the duvet. He could lie in the warm, looking out at the rest of the furniture.

There was a table which supported a very old computer and vast piles of folders. Pens were strewn everywhere, along with pencils, felt tips and poster paints, for Tom liked drawing, and the walls were covered in startling pictures of rockets and bombs. There was a bookcase, too, and the shelves were bending under the weight of the books. It was jammed against a wardrobe that was almost bursting with jeans, T-shirts and too-big sweaters, everything scented with Tom's unique mixture of smells.

The only thing that was hung up neatly was a black blazer edged in a thin red stripe. On the front was a gold badge in the shape of a lion, and a serious-looking tie was looped over the shoulders. It had a forbidding, funereal look.

"Don't," said Tom.

He had followed Spider's gaze, and the dog noticed an alarmingly serious edge to his voice.

"Are you going to chew things?" he said. "I know dogs do, but if you chew any of my school stuff, we're dead. Both of us. That's 'uniform', that is, and it cost us a fortune. In fact…"

He pushed the wardrobe door closed, and wedged it shut with a slipper.

"There. Let's forget about it."

He rubbed Spider's head.

"We go back next week. There's been a holiday, but school starts again soon—and I won't be taking you."

Spider blinked thoughtfully, and licked Tom's thumb.

"You'd hate it, anyway—it's scary. You're going to stay in the garden because Dad will be sleeping. You'll have access to the kitchen, too. Phil's at college, so he comes and goes. What we need to do, though, is sort out all the basics. You seem a pretty good dog to me—I mean, you do what you're told already. But you need wide open spaces, don't you? And that means the lead."

Spider licked each one of Tom's fingers then, and started to bite them.

Tom laughed, and played with his ears.

"You're such a monster," he said. "Dad thinks you ought to be sleeping downstairs, and I suppose you should, really. But the way I look at it is that you're only young, and you're not used to being on your own yet—how could you be? So for the first week or two, while we're adjusting, I'm going smuggle you up here. We can protect each other, OK? But we've got to be careful. No barking, unless there's a real emergency. And there won't be."

The very next morning, Tom produced a collar.

It was blue, with two metal rings. One held a tag on which various numbers were engraved, and the other was shaped to receive the clip of a strong leather leash. Spider wore it with pride, and Tom led him down the hallway to the front door. When he opened it, the dog realized that the moment had come: the outside world was before him again, and it was so different from the garden. He darted on to the pavement, tripping over his own paws. Tom laughed, and restrained him as firmly as he dared. The next moment, they were making their way down the street together, past doors of every colour. There were cars, nose to tail, and so many poles and posts that the dog was soon dizzy. They went past a boarded-up shop, and a house enveloped in the scent of exotic spices. Crossing the road, Tom turned into an alleyway which became a labyrinth of paths and passages. Spider forged ahead, determined to lose himself, and before long they came to a pair of tall metal gates.

"OK," said Tom. "This is the park."

They were both out of breath and panting.

"Sit."

Spider was astonished. The gates were open, inviting him into a vast expanse of the greenest grass he'd ever seen, and yet Tom's hand was pressing at his haunches. He twisted, and tried to run.

"No, Spider! No." Tom pushed him down again. "Sit down, please. We're doing this together. We're learning to be patient."

The dog sat down, wondering why they had to rest. Tom had a firm hold of his collar, and he couldn't resist pulling away again. He ducked, and got a paw over Tom's arm, and he was about to squirm his way to freedom when he was showered in gravel. A bicycle had skidded to a halt, just missing them both.

"Wow," said a voice. "Tommy Lipman."

Spider bounded forward, and Tom was jerked off balance so that he ended up on the ground, his feet entangled in the lead. The bicycle came closer still, its grinning rider staring down at the confusion.

"What have you got there?" he asked, laughing. "My God, Lipman—where did you get that?"

"Hi, Rob," said Tom. "What are you doing?"

"None of your business."

"You don't live round here."

"I'm seeing friends, Lipman. You wouldn't understand that because you don't have any. Seriously, though, what is that thing?"

"He's my new dog."

"No way," said Rob. "You can't call that thing a dog! Look at its mouth, man. Is it a boy or a girl? Or doesn't it know?"

"He's a boy."

"Really? You've checked, have you?"

Rob was still smiling, but Spider sensed Tom's unease.

"Check again, Lipman!" cried the boy. "You get a bit confused about gender, don't you? And we're still not sure what you are yet. Hey, don't walk away, buddy—I'm talking to you."

"We're busy, Rob. See you next week."

"Oh, Lipman, you're so asking for it."

"Goodbye, Rob."

"I'll see you soon. You can't get away from us, you know: we'll be waiting."

Spider was totally bewildered. Tom had started to run, and the boy on the bike was following. He was shouting questions, too, but Tom wasn't answering—he was trying to sort out the lead, which had become knotted again. Suddenly, Spider was free, for the end that had been looped round his master's wrist flipped on to the grass.

The dog bounded sideways as a bolt of energy burst inside him. Tom went to hold him back, but it was so easy to dodge, and Spider was off like a rocket, racing over the grass in an unstoppable sprint. If Tom's friend was still with them, Spider didn't hear him. He was curving to the right, with Tom in hot pursuit. In the distance he'd spied a speck of grey, and he knew just what it was: another dog was in the park.

Tom yelled his name, so Spider raced back, swerving out of his reach. He tripped over his lead, and somersaulted neatly back on to his feet, galloping towards his new playmate. They veered off, side by side, towards a distant hedge, and slipped straight through it. Tom's cries grew faint and disappeared altogether under the splashing of a brook. Spider was paddling for the first time in his life, feeling mud between his toes and water on his fur—he didn't notice when his companion left him.

He clambered up a bank into thick brambles. Rich smells poured from a tunnel that something wild had bored into the undergrowth. Spider plunged into it, for this was so much better than the garden he was used to. He was soon lost in a maze. When he emerged, minutes later, he found himself in a whole new area of woodland, and now there were pine needles under his paws.

He trotted into a clearing, hoping Tom was keeping up. But there was no sign or scent of him, so he ran back eagerly. The park was some way behind, but he sensed the way, for there was a path ahead which led to gates and a road—he could see a line of parked cars identical to the ones he'd passed earlier. When he trotted along beside them, the street looked very like the one he lived in—but there was no boarded-up shop, and he noticed there were sets of iron railings which were unfamiliar.

Spider sat down.

He wondered if Tom would come the other way and meet him further along. He set off again, full of hope, but the only human being he could see was someone pushing a pram. At last, Spider saw a boy, and broke into a run—but he soon saw that it wasn't Tom, or his friend the cyclist. He slowed again, and was immediately distracted by a telegraph pole. Having snuffled around that, he realized it would be best to retrace his steps. The problem was, he wasn't sure which direction that meant, so he turned, and turned again. The pram was coming closer, its wheels rumbling. Spider backed away, and that's when he heard the awful howl of a siren—it was a wave of sound accompanied by flashing lights and squealing tyres. An engine backfired, loud as a gunshot, and Spider bolted.

All the driver saw was a blur of black and white.

He stamped on his brakes, and lost control at once. Somebody screamed, but the noise was lost in a rending screech of metal, and an explosion of glass. Spider knew he was dead: his short life flashed in front of his eyes, with a quick vision of Tom, followed by his bed in the attic room. He glimpsed the silver cat he'd once stared at, but the back end of the van was now swinging towards him and he could do nothing but cringe in terror.

Somehow, the back wheel came to a juddering, steaming halt a few centimetres from his nose.

The driver gazed down through the broken window, open-mouthed.

Spider backed away.

A hand grabbed his collar, and he twisted round, hoping with all his heart that it would be Tom. It wasn't: a woman had stepped into the road, and he was caught. She was pulling at his tag, and more people were gathering round, looking down at him with grave faces. Instinct told him he was in serious trouble.

4

It was Phil who came to collect him.

When they got home, Tom was waiting, and Spider just managed to get his paws up and lick the boy's face. The boy tried to hold on to him, but they were separated at once. Spider smelled the unsettling scent of fear, and it dawned on him that it was Tom who was going to be punished. He crept up the stairs to the bedroom he loved, and that was when the shouting started.

Tom's dad was furious. How had the boy dropped the lead? Why had they even gone to the park, and why couldn't Tom be trusted with the simplest thing? The dog got on to the bed, trembling, and curled up on the duvet as the shouting got louder. The boy's voice was shaking as he tried to reply.

Phil said something, but Tom's dad was talking about money and debt and the need to show responsibility, especially now, when things were harder than they'd ever been.

Tom started to sob, and Spider lay there, panting in fear.

"Wow," said a voice.

The dog whined miserably, and looked up.

"Oh my word, little dog. What have you done?"

Spider whined again. He looked all around the bedroom, for he'd been certain he was alone. That was when the skylight creaked, and he heard a soft, self-satisfied chuckle. He knew at once who'd spoken: a tiny black spider was dangling from the ceiling where the window frame was broken, and as he watched, it lowered itself to a few centimetres above his head. He saw the eyes he remembered so well: Thread had found him again, and was soon right on his nose.

"Good to see you," it said quietly. "What have you been up to, eh? Something bad, by the sound of it. Something stupid?"

"I don't know what happened."

"Don't you?"

"No."

"I think you do. I can tell truth from lies, you know—and you're not being honest."

"Look, it wasn't my fault," said Spider. "I got lost, and I panicked! I just… ran for it."

"Where did you go?"

"Through a wood and out, into a road, and—"

"Into the road, eh? Ah, that's your nature, you see."

"Is it?"

"You're out of control. You're what's called a 'bad dog'."

"I'm not bad! I just didn't think about it, Thread. I was looking for home and I got confused."

"Where's home, though? You're an unwanted mongrel, don't forget. This isn't your home."

"It is. I think it is."

"It *was*, perhaps. But you're on trial, remember? What they really wanted was a cat."

Spider stood up, and found that he was barking.

"No," he said. "They did *not* want a cat—or Tom didn't. And they wouldn't do anything hasty. I mean, OK, I've just caused a problem, but…"

"What?"

Spider blinked and shook his head. He became aware of his protruding tooth and tried to close his mouth properly, turning a complete circle on the bed.

"Oh my goodness," he said. "This is dreadful."

"It's the end, I'd say. It's a disaster."

"I *am* to blame."

"You certainly are."

"Tom's going to be held responsible, isn't he? For the damage, I mean."

"Was there much?"

"There was glass everywhere! And bashed-in cars…"

Spider closed his eyes as he remembered how the van had been spun round and smashed. He shook himself harder, and the spider clung to his fur, laughing.

"Look," said the dog. "You're not helping me, Thread. Why are you even here? Did you follow me?"

"You didn't notice?"

"No!"

"Ah, so you're thick-skinned and insensitive, too. I had second thoughts, buddy—just as you were leaving. I jumped on to your back, and here I am. That window up there is perfect, so I've landed on my feet, so to speak."

"You're going to stay there?"

"Why not?"

"You can't just move in! This is Tom's bedroom."

"Mine, too, dog. I've made myself comfortable, and the food's been good so far. Tell me what happened, though—what made you bolt?"

Spider stared at the little spider, and its eyes gazed back into his own. He flopped down on to his side, and told the whole, sad story from beginning to end. He talked about the park, and the strange boy on the bike. He described the grey dog, and the tunnels, and when he finally got to the carnage in the road he realized that, once again, Thread was laughing.

"What?" said Spider. "What's so funny?"

"I'm thinking about Tom. How old is he?"

"Eleven."

"Yes. And he's out of control—like you."

Spider rolled over suddenly, rubbing his head hard on the nearest pillow.

"Get off me, Thread! That boy's done nothing wrong!"

"Oh, come on, dog," cried the spider, shifting to Spider's ear. "He's a total disaster. Look at this room, for a start. You can tell a lot by the habitat, and that kid is plain uncivilized. The whole house is a tip, to be honest—not that it bothers me, because I thrive on mess. But I'd say this family is unstable—where's the mother?"

"I don't know. I've wondered that too."

"There's a photograph on the shelf. It's been turned to the wall, so what's happening there? And why is she calling him every day?"

"What are you talking about?"

"You don't listen! I keep my ears open, and I can tell you something: she calls him every day, and he won't even speak to her. This is a dysfunctional family, from top to bottom. Get out while you can—you're better off as a stray."

Spider let out a short, agonized whine. "No! Where would I go?"

"Somewhere else. They'll be calling the dogs' home any minute, and you don't want to end up there."

"A dogs' home? What's a dogs' home?"

"It's a kind of prison. The pets go in, but they don't often come out."

"That's not possible! Tom likes me, Thread. He loves me—"

"But Dad's the big boss, isn't he?"

"Maybe, but—"

"He's got a short fuse, too, and he won't be listening to the kid. You just pray you don't end up in a river, because I've seen that happen, too. A brick round your neck, and you're stuck in a sack. One big splash, and down you go. You could even face the lab if they decide to sell you."

Spider blinked.

"You know what the lab is?" said Thread quietly.

"No."

"Boy, oh boy, you're green. Welcome to the world, dog—you're going to have to learn about it. A lab is a laboratory, and they're the worst of the worst. I don't want to scare you, but I've spoken to bugs that have been inside them, and they tell me the whole story—it's another place for rejects like you. Lines of animals, chained up in cages. That's when the white coats come by, and you have to stand there and take it. Shampoo in the eyes, electric shocks... Cigarette smoke! Crikey, they force it down your lungs till your fur drops out—*that* gives you cancer, and they sit there making notes. Dog after dog, so I'm told—hundreds of them—all puffing away with their paws wired together."

"That's impossible—"

"It's reality, friend, so don't shoot the messenger. I told you when we met: I'm the truth teller. You want fairy tales? Find a book, and learn to read."

"No," said Spider. "I'm not listening any more. Tom wouldn't send me away—we've bonded."

The spider laughed again, and wound itself upwards.

"I'd make a run for it, puppy dog. I can hear footsteps, so you'd better make your mind up. Fight or flight, those are the options. That's nature, and creatures like you—"

"It's Tom! He's coming."

"With the brick, I'll bet. Get ready—"

"No! And I'm never running off again. Ever!"

Thread disappeared into the skylight above, and Spider found he was trembling all over. The fur on his back was sticking up as if he'd been electrocuted, and when Tom appeared in the doorway he found he was cowering. He moved back against the wall and lifted a paw.

Tom stopped.

"Oh, Spider," he said.

Spider hung his head. He couldn't look up, for the boy's voice was so full of tears, and his face was wet.

"Spider," he said. "I'm sorry."

The dog waited, too confused to even whimper. He could hear the pain, and it dawned on him that this really was the end. Tom had already had enough—he'd been let down by the one he loved, and the experiment was over. He sat on the bed wearily, and looked at his pet.

"It wasn't your fault," said the boy. "Come here—come on. It was my mistake, OK? I should never have dropped the lead. I nearly got you killed, but I didn't think. I just... It was that kid, Rob Tayler. I hate him, Spider. He was yelling at me—all the usual stuff—so I just got confused. And I... I let go."

Tom drew Spider into his arms.

"I really thought I'd lost you, boy. I ran after you and... You're the only dog I've ever owned. I didn't know what I was doing, and Dad's so angry because we're broke again. We're always, always broke, and he says he should never have got you, but I told him..."

Spider managed a lick. He crept closer, and felt both Tom's arms round his neck.

"I love you, OK?" said the boy softly.

He drew the dog on to his lap.

"Dad says we should have got a cat, but that's not true. Cats are selfish, horrible things—I hate them. We're going to put this behind us and show him what an amazing, wonderful dog you are—because you *are*. He'll see it one day, Spider. You're the best, and we'll show him."

5

From that day on, Spider tried extra hard.

He would wake up early, and wait for Tom to come to life. School had started, so five mornings a week there was a careful ritual as the boy transformed himself. Spider gazed as he pulled on black trousers and a white shirt. The tie came next, intricately knotted and painstakingly adjusted. It was black, with red, diagonal bars. Over that went the sombre jacket, and Spider would watch as Tom buttoned it so the golden lion gleamed over his heart. Five minutes later, he'd comb his hair and pat Spider's head. He'd leave the house, and the dog would trot off to the back garden.

A fence had been erected halfway down to keep him safe, and

he could move freely in and out of the kitchen. Phil appeared around lunchtime with food, and Spider combined sleep and exercise quite happily until Tom returned. Then up he went to the boy's bedroom, his paws drumming joyfully, and Tom peeled the same uniform off to put it carefully back in the wardrobe. He then sat down at his desk, and only when he'd completed a full two hours of concentrated homework did he look up and smile.

"Done," he would say.

Spider would be on his feet.

"You ready, boy? Let's hit the park."

When he heard those words, Spider would leap up in a corkscrew of pleasure. Ten minutes later they'd be through the gates, looking out at the expanse of grass.

The dog did his best to obey Tom's commands promptly, and they settled into a routine that seemed to make everybody happy. At first, disobeying an order made Tom laugh, but it soon led to frustration and repetition. It was easier, in the end, to sit when instructed, and come when called. "Heel!" was the most difficult thing, and they practised that for what seemed like hours. "Heel!" meant "Calm down! Go slow!"—and that was totally against Spider's quick, bright nature.

The park soon became a gloriously familiar place, as were the streets around it. They explored the woods a little, too, though Spider was always on the lead. Days turned to weeks, and finally the moment came: once again, he was to be given unlimited freedom. He understood that his collar would remain fixed to his neck. The lead, however, could be unhooked in a second. As Tom bent down and took hold, Spider knew he was facing the most important test of his life so far. He could feel the boy getting anxious.

Suddenly, the lead was off—and Spider just managed not to run. The boy walked backwards slowly. He called Spider's name, and Spider leapt forward, straight to him. This caused Tom a quite remarkable amount of pleasure and relief, so they did it again and again. It became a regular thing: they'd get to the park, and Spider found that once he'd performed that simple trick, he was trusted. The trust meant he could go where he wanted, so off he'd go to frisk with the other dogs—and he soon had dozens of friends.

He was constantly astounded at the variety around him. There were creatures twice his size, but what intrigued him were the ones that were so tiny they looked like toys. There were bald dogs and hairy dogs, and a particularly nervous creature who looked just like a lamb. For a while, Spider was fascinated by an Alsatian who talked earnestly about his career in the police force. There was an old greyhound, too, who would totter unsteadily off the path, before standing absolutely still with her eyes closed. She talked so quietly that Spider had to put his ear close to her nose, and she'd whisper about her time on some racetrack. When he got back home he'd think about all he had heard, and wonder in his heart if he should be catching criminals, or competing in complicated sports before cheering crowds. Most animals liked to talk about themselves, he noticed, but if a dog ever said "So then, what are you?", he was a little nervous about answering.

"A pet," he'd say.

"I can see that. What kind, though?"

"No kind, really. Just a pet."

*

Tom seemed happy enough, and that was the important thing. They played with sticks, and they played with balls. The sun would be sinking, but they would always squeeze another few minutes out of the day to run, jump and wrestle. Tom would throw; Spider would catch. There was a wonderful balance, and a sense that the game might never end.

"Find it, Spider! Fetch!"

Wherever the object fell, Spider would be there. He'd tease Tom the way Tom teased him, but he'd always return things in the end and the boy would hurl them away again. Spider found that some nights he would dream of sticks and chase them in his sleep. More than once he'd wake up with his legs pumping, astonished that he wasn't in the park at all. The duvet would be on the floor, and Tom would be curled on his side, thumb in mouth.

The only complication was the boy on the bike, who often reappeared at weekends. Sometimes he came alone, and sometimes he had friends with him. What worried Spider was that his conversation always seemed to make Tom nervous.

"Who cuts your hair, Lipman?" the boy said, on one occasion. "You're as ugly as your dog."

"I do."

"That makes sense, then—saving money. I thought you were a little girl when I first saw you—and, oh, you're running away again. We're coming for you soon, you know: me and Marcus. We're going to train you properly. Teach you some manners."

Spider began to feel like a bodyguard.

Tom still smuggled him up to his room every night, and Spider would curl into the crook of his master's knees, and, just occasionally, when he felt mischievous, he'd nibble at the boy's toes. Tom, meanwhile, got into the habit of bringing him toys to chew. Spider's near-death experience with the van receded further and further into the chasms of memory. One particular night, the boy was stroking him as usual, and Spider was leaning into the caress, waiting for the head scratch. It came at last, and went on for two of the nicest minutes of the day. He snuggled down, and Tom turned the light out. Minutes later, he was fast asleep, his heartbeat slowing until it thumped in the same, slow rhythm as Spider's. The dog squirmed a little closer, enjoying the harmony, and was just about to settle properly when he made a grave mistake. He looked up at the skylight.

Two eyes were staring through the glass, and they didn't belong to Thread. Spider jolted to his feet and discovered that his tail was rigid.

The eyes were luminous green.

They didn't blink and, as they came closer, he realized that he'd seen them before, weeks and weeks ago, when he'd lived in a box. He recognized the whiskers and the ears and the slim shoulders: it was the silver cat who'd perched on the window sill, and all he wanted was to chase her.

She was on the roof, of course.

Spider stared up helplessly, wondering if she was really flesh and blood—she appeared phosphorescent in the moonlight, and a gentle breeze stirred the fur all along her spine. Her ribcage tapered to a delicate waist, and her legs were long. Her eyes widened, and when she tilted her head gently to the right, the pupils flashed and changed colour.

Spider felt a wild electricity and started to shake.

Tom put out a hand, sleepily, to stroke and reassure him.

"Stay," he mumbled. Then he groaned, "No, sir. It's in my locker..."

Spider hardly heard him.

The cat studied the dog and lifted her chin. Then she put up a paw and revealed sharp, even claws. Spider growled, for they were talons of polished steel, and they'd emerged with mechanical precision. She licked her nose with the neatest, cleanest, pinkest tongue he'd ever seen. The eyes were darkening to jet black, and as he whined again they turned to fiery amber.

"Spider," she said softly. "Is that really you?"

Spider nodded. "Yes."

"Oh, forgive me. What must you think? Don't speak, though..."

The dog couldn't have spoken even if he'd had something to say. He was panting and trying to swallow a mouthful of saliva.

"You are Spider, aren't you? The puppy I was once so close to, weeks ago? And this is... Oh my, this is forbidden, I know, but I had to find you, Spider. We need to talk..."

Spider managed to reply, but it was a husky whimper. "You know my name?"

"I saw you on that beastly leash. I heard you being called."

"When?"

"Yesterday. Today. Every day! Spider, don't you remember me?"

"Yes, of course!"

"Oh, thank you. You don't know what that means to me—to be noticed and remembered. But I should go, shouldn't I? Dogs and cats, cats and dogs—there's a certain... distance between us, and rightly so."

"You were in the garden, weren't you? I wanted to chase you."

"Of course you did."

"I still do!"

"Ah, you're so natural, angel. It's your nature, your... instinct."

"Did you follow me home? How did you find me?"

"I followed my heart. I just wanted to see you one more time. I'm a wanderer, Spider—like you, perhaps, when you're not on that dreadful leather string, dragged about like a slave. We're chasing each other, it seems! But, no... No, my dear. I see your master needs you, and I should leave. Isn't too late, though."

"Too late for what?"

"To stop what's so inevitable. Oh, when can we meet?"

"Tomorrow," said Spider. "I'll be in the garden—"

"Impossible, no."

"The park, then—late afternoon?"

"I'll be gone by morning, and... You must forget me. I'm a wild, crazy fool to even speak to you—to bare my heart—but... won't you take pity on a lonely soul? Climb up, Spider! Will you do that for me? Now?"

"How? I can't really climb."

"I think you can. There's a cat inside you somewhere. Isn't there?"

"Is there?"

"You haven't felt it, struggling within you?"

"I don't know..."

"You have a cat's tooth, you know—I can see it. And we share a soul, Spider, so why not try? Brave heart, we can only fail."

Spider slipped off the bed on to the floor. He heard Tom turn and moan quietly, so he licked the boy's hand, then he stepped up on to the chair beside the desk.

"I might be able to get a *bit* higher," he said. "I could do that, possibly, if you could open the window more. Stay where you are—and mind the spider."

"What spider?"

"There's a web up there. Don't break it."

Spider clambered up on to the desk and looked around for footholds. It wasn't going to be easy, but a jump and scramble might do it, if he got his claws on the shelf above his head. He launched himself, and, amazingly, without dislodging anything at all, he forced his way up to the flat top of the wardrobe, where he found himself pressed beneath the ceiling. He pushed his snout to the window frame, and the cat backed off, gazing at him out of gemstone eyes.

"Can you open it a bit wider?" hissed Spider. "If you can press down, the whole thing should swing."

The cat shook her head. "We're fools, you know," she said. "This isn't wise."

"What isn't?"

"Are we tempting fate? You're strong, though. I can see it!"

"I'm here now," said Spider. "This is tricky, but I'll give it a go..."

He got a paw on to the glass and, sure enough, the whole skylight rotated downwards, leaving him a gap the width of his own body. He jumped again, knowing that if he paused to think about it he'd fall straight down on to the carpet. He floundered, and squeezed on to a slope of wet, chilly roof tiles. His paws slipped over them, but at least he was out. His back legs kicked out by instinct and he got some leverage from the edge of the frame. Thread's webs caught his fur, and he thought of the little spider—how furious it would be!

Twisting and pushing, Spider was up and free—and that was

when he realized with horror that the roof was dangerously steep. Again, he scratched at the tiles, and again his claws skittered straight over them. The cat reversed quickly, watching with wide, passionate eyes. Spider slid downwards, away from her, and knew he was in real trouble. A new instinct saved him: he splayed himself out on all fours, and the friction of his fur acted as a painful brake. He stretched out absolutely flat and came to rest sideways, just above the gutter. Below was the abyss: a sheer drop to the hard, unforgiving pavement. He glimpsed Phil's moped and felt his stomach turn over.

The cat padded carefully down towards him and licked a paw.

"That was heroic," she purred. "That was catlike, Spider—catlike in its daring."

Spider blinked.

"I think it was a mistake," he said.

His rear end was hanging in space, and he could feel it dragging the rest of him down. There was no way of getting back to the skylight, and he was about to fall.

"You're so bold," said the cat. "No dog I've ever met has had such courage. I know what people say—that dogs are fearless and loyal by nature—but I'm afraid that's rarely true. The dogs I've met are violent, selfish, shallow creatures—do you know what I mean?"

"No," said Spider. "I'm not sure of anything right now."

"Oh, you're so honest!"

"I mean, wait. I'm not sure I can stay like this—I really am about to fall off the roof."

"Please don't!"

"I don't want to, but—"

"Where shall we go? Where can we talk?"

"Look, I need help."

"We should find somewhere warm."

"Could you steady me, perhaps? Can you reach my tail?"

"I'm not strong, Spider—you can see that. I've always relied upon the strength of others. Oh, I can be quick, yes—but in many ways I'm just a helpless kitten, and the world is so cruel."

"I really do need help here. It's urgent."

"Don't leave me, Spider! What a waste it would be…"

Spider was feeling sick: one leg was now floating in thin air. He managed to force his front paw on to the metal edge of the gutter and brought the leg that was adrift slowly back to safety. Then, by leaning heavily to one side, he was able to worm his way slowly upwards, like a slug. A television aerial was his target: if he could reach that, he could perch on its broad metal base.

The cat watched, moving with him, just out of reach. She passed above, and Spider kept his eyes on hers.

By the time he made it, he was panting and shivering.

"You're amazing," said the cat.

"I feel ill."

"You have cat in your blood, you see! That's what I told everyone, and that's what drew me to you. Let's go up to the chimney stack— I'll show you my domain."

"Seriously, I'm not sure I can. I'm heavier than you."

"Watch me."

The cat jumped, and in three quick leaps she was at the top of the roof, where the slates met the brickwork.

Spider gulped and resisted the terrible urge to look down. He fixed his eyes on a narrow strip of lead: it was a seal against the weather, and he stepped on to it, knowing that any delay would be fatal. His paws found their grip, and he jumped and

39

ran at the same time, claws scraping as his elbows and knees worked together. He kept his eyes on the chimney, and soon he was squeezing himself up into a flat, sheltered recess. For the first time, he felt secure enough to relax, and though he could feel his heart knocking against his ribcage, he was thrilled by his achievement. What alarmed him now, though, was that the cat he'd been following was actually one of many. There were two further down, and another three perched on the ridge. They were all watching Spider in silence, and as he gazed about him another sauntered close and winked at him.

Had they all gathered for the view? It was spectacular, for the lines of houses criss-crossed under a vast cavern of stars. Spider could see the park, and just beyond it the tower of a church. There was a tangle of railway tracks behind, gleaming silver, and they seemed to pass under a long snake of road that rose to a huge, hurtling flyover where lights blazed in an unending stream. It was siphoning cars out into an unknown world: some were circling, while others darted like fish. There was a soft, constant roar. When Spider looked up again, he saw an aeroplane drifting towards the moon.

"You see?" said his companion. "The world is wider than you thought."

"It certainly is."

"We're close to the sea. Did you know that? We could go there now if you wanted to. Are we fools, Spider?"

"I really don't know. Who are your friends?"

"Oh, I have my followers," she whispered. "They wanted to see you because I'd said so much about you. But aren't you ever going to ask my name?"

Spider nodded. "What is it?"

"Guess."

"I can't."

"No? Look at my fur, and think of poetry…"

"Princess, perhaps?"

There was a chorus of mewing, which the first cat silenced with a hiss.

"No," she said. "You're charming, and you know it—but it's not Princess." She narrowed her eyes. "I'll give you a clue, if you like. I wouldn't normally offer up my secrets, but listen to my riddle: I'm a creature of the dark that comes out at night."

"I don't know—the stars?"

"Bigger than that, Spider. What's that big, shiny white thing?"

"I thought of that when I first saw you. Moonlight? Is that your name?"

The cat was nodding, and those listening rattled their claws. That was when Spider heard the tinkle of a tiny bell, and saw that his new friend wore a neat red collar. She padded towards him, and he thought how unattractive his own one was. He tried to conceal his projecting tooth, and suddenly she was beside him, pressing herself into the rough brickwork so they were shoulder to shoulder. Spider leant against her, feeling the warmth of her fur. For the first time he caught the scent of his companion, and he was utterly confused.

"You might have been right," he said quietly.

"About what?"

"There could be cat inside me. I'm a mongrel, after all: do you think it's possible?"

"Darling, it's certain," said Moonlight. "That must be why I needed to find you. As you say, you have the legs and head of an ugly mongrel-dog, but inside you have the soul of a cat. Why not?"

"I don't know. But I ought to be with Tom—"

"Who's Tom?"

"Tom. My owner, my master—"

"Oh, the little boy in the park! Nobody owns you, Spider."

"Tom does."

"Not true," said Moonlight. "He *thinks* he owns you because of that evil chain. But how can a spirit like yours ever be owned or tamed? Don't humble yourself!"

"You're owned yourself, though—by that lady."

"Which lady?"

"In the place I was born. The old lady who looked after me—"

"I told you, Spider: no. We are creatures of the night."

"So who looks after you?"

"I look after myself, and I roam free."

The cat closed her eyes. She let her tail drift across her nose and moved her mouth close to Spider's ear. He felt her whiskers on his cheek, and had to master an urge to grab her with his paws.

"Listen to me," she said softly. "To be owned is to be enslaved. Don't waste your life on a heartless boy. Come with us, and see the world!"

"Oh, I couldn't do that. Tom trusts me now. He goes to a school, Moonlight, but I don't think he's happy there. He gets tired—even tearful, sometimes."

"Boys stick together, Spider. They're like wolves in a pack. They're cruel and noisy—lazy, too. Why, that boy down there will only need you for a few more weeks—or a few months, perhaps—and what then? What then, when you've given him your heart? He'll forget you and go his own wicked way. Oh, I shouldn't be talking like this. I know I shouldn't—what right do

I have? I'm just a foolish cat, but I've learnt to trust my instincts, Spider. I don't want a brave, noble heart like yours to get hurt. He will leave you, and suddenly you'll be alone."

"But what would I do without him? How would I live?"

The cat pushed her nose against Spider's and purred.

"With me," she said.

"No."

"Why not?"

"Moonlight, you're scaring me. Where would we go? How would we survive?"

"We'd go wild! The earth would be our pillow, and the stars would cover us. We'd walk the open road and be as free as birds. Oh, I *use* houses—of course I do—but the day I have an owner is the day I'd swallow poison. Let me go."

Spider shook his head in dismay. "This is terrible," he said. "I don't know what to do."

"Of course you don't."

"What am I? I thought I was a normal dog."

"You're *you*, Spider. And it's wrong of me—so terribly wrong, I just can't bear it sometimes—to see a creature full of hope, squandering his life when he could run with cats! But now I've seen you. I've shown you off, so I must leave you to yourself."

"Moonlight, why?"

"Promise me something, though, angel! Promise me you won't forget this moment. Don't speak! Let's just listen to the night."

Spider sat absolutely still with his eyes tight shut.

The cat pressed her cheek against his, and a minute passed.

"Shall I see you again?" Moonlight whispered, nipping him gently.

"I hope so. You know where I live."

"Then this isn't goodbye. I shall return, sweet thing—and perhaps we shall make music."

With that, she turned away.

Spider watched her leaping back up to the ridge. She padded swiftly through the other cats, and though Spider tried to follow, it was impossible. She turned and the whole pack looked at him, their eyes sparkling with a mixture of menace and fascination. Moonlight led them away, and they disappeared over the rooftops.

Spider whined and forced himself to stay still. He saw them once more, with Moonlight at the front, a streak of silver racing along the roofline and arcing into the darkness. He gazed and whimpered, desperate to follow—but they didn't reappear.

The dog turned then, and licked his lips. He felt the tooth that protruded and looked at his black and white legs splayed out on the slates. His ears were in his eyes, and he had never felt more lopsided. Worst of all, he had no idea how he was going to get home without killing himself. He couldn't see the skylight any more, and the whole town seemed to be spinning slowly beneath him. He had lost all sense of direction.

Tom woke up early because he was cold.

The first thing he noticed was that the weight he was used to, down at the end of the bed, was gone. It was a weight he'd come to love, for it pressed its heat into the crooks of his knees while it fought for extra space. The bed felt wrong without it. There was a cold breeze too, for the window above his head was gaping open. Tom's bedroom had no radiator, so he was shivering.

It made sense to get up and pull on a jersey, and that's when he noticed the door was still closed. If the door was shut, Spider couldn't have passed through it—and that meant his best friend must still be in the room. Tom saw at once that this wasn't possible, for there were no hiding places. The idea that he had somehow jumped vertically upwards out of the skylight was ridiculous, so that meant, logically, that his dad (or Phil) had entered his room in the night without waking him and carried Spider away.

He crept downstairs, listening for movement. The house was silent, and he had the very strong sense that it was Spider-less. He padded into the kitchen, and—sure enough—the basket was empty. The back door was closed, so Tom was forced to sit down at the table and face the fact that there was no explanation. He was now seriously worried. Ideally, he would have woken up his father and asked him what had happened. That was unwise, however, as his father had just got to bed and would be seriously cross if anyone disturbed him. Phil wouldn't be down for a while, so he resigned himself to an impatient wait.

Tom showered to get warm, and went back upstairs to get dressed. It was a schoolday, so that meant the usual too-big uniform. He had two white shirts, and they were both dirty. He pulled the cleaner one on, tucking it in firmly. Without a belt his trousers would have fallen straight down to his ankles, and his blazer was more like an overcoat. His clownish appearance amused the other boys, who had mocked him all year without mercy. Even the tie felt ridiculous. Tom pulled the jersey back on and walked slowly down to the kitchen.

The house had lost its soul.

The phone rang at seven forty-five, as it did most mornings. He listened as the answerphone service cut in, inviting the caller to leave a message. The silence that followed was a long one, and he stood with his eyes closed. His mother spoke, softly, and after three words he turned the machine off.

At ten past eight, the door opened.

"Phil," said Tom, "have you seen Spider?"

"Of course not. And what are you doing here at this time? You should have left by now."

"I'm talking to you, about my dog."

"You'll be late again."

"He's gone missing, Phil. Someone's taken him or he's escaped."

Phil laughed. "Have you checked the garden?"

"The door's locked. How would he get out?"

"I've no idea. You should've bought yourself a fish, mate, and kept it safe in a bowl. That dog's causing nothing but trouble."

Tom bit his tongue and stifled a scream. Phil brought his idiotic goldfish up whenever he could, claiming it had a distinct personality. Tom despised the creature.

"Look," he said quietly. "You locked up last night. Did you lock all the doors?"

"Of course."

"You forget sometimes."

"Rarely."

"So, if you definitely locked up, Spider couldn't have got out. That means someone's broken into my bedroom and taken him."

"Your dad, you mean? Why would your dad steal Spider?"

"I don't know. Because he doesn't like him?"

"Tom, he's exhausted at the moment. He's on shift work. The shift has changed—"

"I know that. He was going on about it."

"So he's not going to muck about stealing dogs. Why is Spider sleeping in your room anyway?"

"He's lonely."

"Really? You're breaking the rules."

47

"He needs looking after, Phil. He's missing his family."

"Really."

Phil was looking at the answerphone and its winking red light.

"Has your mum phoned?" he said.

"No."

"That's a message. Is it her?"

"Perhaps," said Tom. "I don't know, and I don't care."

"She just wants to speak to you, man—and you can't keep avoiding it. You need to be brave, all right?"

"I need to find Spider, Phil. That's what I'm thinking about, and I haven't got time for anything else."

"I'll look for him, all right? You need to get going."

"Why? I hate the place—you know I do. I don't want to go there, and... I don't see why I should."

Phil sighed and sat down. He played with his keys for a moment, and Tom stared at the table.

"I thought things were improving," Phil said. "You told me it was getting better."

"Did I?" Tom snorted, and put his head in his hands.

He felt a prickling in his nose, which signalled the onset of tears. He knew he wouldn't cry, though, because he had crying under strict control. He pressed his teeth together and blinked: sure enough, the moment passed, and his eyes were dry. He didn't normally get tearful in his own kitchen, and he was angry with himself.

"What are they saying?" asked Phil.

"Nothing. The usual."

"Then you need to talk to someone. Or your dad does."

"To say what? I'm at the wrong school, with the wrong people."

"And the scholarship?"

"Stuff it."

"No. You have a tutor, don't you?"

"She's useless."

"Then we'll see the head of year, or the head. There is no way you should put up with any kind of crap."

"Why not?" said Tom. "I put up with yours."

He walked out of the room, leaving Phil standing in shocked silence.

Tom climbed to the top of the house and packed the bag he should have packed the previous evening. He checked he had his homework and his diary and his pencil case, and at the last moment remembered it was PE, which meant he needed his kit, which hadn't been washed—it was still screwed up in a carrier bag. He exchanged his jersey for the blazer, but even as he put his pen in the pocket he realized he'd been serious: he wasn't going to school. He could not sit in a classroom while Spider was lost, so he would skip a day. Instead, he would scour the streets in every direction, walking till his smart new shoes fell to pieces. He would find his friend and bring him home.

Phil was still in the kitchen, nursing a cup of tea.

"Do I talk crap?" he said. "What did you say that for? I'm trying to help you, Tom. I can see you're unhappy—me and your dad."

"I don't need a counsellor, thanks."

"You miss your mum—"

"Really?" interrupted Tom. "You're quite a psychologist, and I'd love to hear more. But right now I'm going to find my dog."

He crossed the hall and pulled the front door open. A bundle of fur exploded at his feet, unfolding into a barking, yelping, licking machine. He was tipped backwards on to the carpet, where he lay in an ecstasy of relief. Spider was in his arms, and the warmth was back: everything in the world had righted itself in an instant. He hugged the dog tight to his chest and nuzzled him. Then he led him back to the kitchen and went to school.

How had Spider found his way down from the rooftops?

He'd never be able to explain, partly because he didn't speak Tom's language, but also because the details were confused in his mind.

One set of slippery slates had looked very like another, and his journey over them had been a nightmare. He remembered that he'd got to a skylight window, only to find that it was the wrong one: he was on a different house entirely. That panicked him, and when he clambered back up to the ridge he was more confused than ever. He tried to do what Moonlight had done, but for him it was like walking a tightrope, and his paws were just too cumbersome. He ended up inching his way along on his belly, moving from chimney to chimney. At last, he found a house with a flat-roofed extension, and though he nearly impaled himself on some vicious spikes, he managed to get down on to a fire escape. There was a gate at the bottom and he had to risk skinning himself, forcing his way through a gap hardly wider than his nose. At one point he got stuck and had to rest for a few minutes, pinched at the hips. After some bone-crushing squirms, he was free, on pavement level at last, and he set about trotting round and round the houses hunting for a landmark.

It was the house that smelt of spices which told him he was close. He moved on, past the boarded-up shop, and caught a whiff of petrol. Phil's moped was by the kerb, outside the familiar yellow door, and though he scratched and whined, it dawned on him that he'd be better off waiting until the morning.

He had sat there for hours, pondering Moonlight's words. Was there cat in his blood? Was that why he'd been drawn to her, the first time he saw her? And was that why he sometimes felt restless? How could he ever abandon Tom? He wasn't a slave.

Cats are selfish, horrible things, he thought. That's what Tom had said, but he hadn't ever met Moonlight.

Spider turned the encounter over in his mind, pondering her words. When the front door finally opened, it was a relief to stop thinking.

7

"So what happened, exactly?" asked Thread. "You busted up my web and made the boy late for school. Full marks, Fido—you're doing well."

"Was he late for school?"

"Of course he was. I hear everything: the school phoned home and woke up his dad. You've done it again, you see."

"I didn't realize. Why do I cause so many problems? I don't mean to, but they just keep happening."

"You know what I think? You're in what's called 'an unsustainable relationship'. Do you know what that means?"

Spider shook his head.

"It means the honeymoon's over, dog. There's no credible

future for the two of you, which is what I said at the start. The first time we met, I told you straight: the set-up is a bad one. You won't get lies from a spider, Spider: we observe the world, and we tell it like it is. You'll find plenty of so-called friends who'll say how wonderful you are, but they're flattering fools. I hear lies and deception every day."

"Who tells you lies?"

"My visitors. Up here, in the web—they're all full of it."

"I don't understand you, Thread—I'm not sure I ever do. What visitors do you get?"

"The bug fraternity. I'm talking about my little clients, OK? Those who check in long-term. You can meet them if you want— they'd be pleased to see a friendly face, even if it's yours."

Spider stared, completely bewildered.

"Use your head," said Thread, chuckling. "How do spiders eat? And, by the way, why did you get called Spider?"

"Because of my legs."

"Of which you have four."

"Yes, but—"

"One at each corner, as is traditional for a quadrupedal dog. You're the least spider-like animal I ever saw, but so be it. That boy's got a lot of problems, so you can't expect him to think rationally. Back to the matter in hand: how does a creature like me get to eat? It's general knowledge."

"You catch things. In a web."

"In the web you put your paw through, yes. You want to meet the gang, then get on the wardrobe."

"I don't think so. I don't want to take any more risks."

"You managed it last night. You were up here in a flash when the cat waved her whiskers. What was all that about?"

"She wanted to talk."

"Oh, I heard what she said."

"What she said to me was private, Thread—and very personal."

"She's playing games, and you need to be careful. Are you coming up or not? Because if you're not, I'll get on with my repairs."

Spider got down from the bed and looked at the skylight. Thread had sailed halfway down, and the window above him seemed high and remote. Nonetheless, he clambered on to Tom's chair and stepped on to the desk. He performed the same, awkward leap, pushing off the convenient shelf and then scrabbling with paws and elbows up to the flat top of the wardrobe. In the daylight he could see just how filthy the window was. There were smears of dirt and complicated nets of grime that spread over the frame. There were webs both old and new, some with torn edges that trailed off sadly and waved in the breeze. Thread crawled to the centre.

"Wow," said Spider. "You keep yourself busy."

"I do."

"Do you make them on your own? It must take ages."

"It does. Some of us work for a living, Spider. Dogs get given stuff out of tins. They get nice big bowls of meaty goodness, and they never even wonder where it comes from. Others have to sweat and toil, and live by their wits."

"What do you catch?"

"Oh, you name it."

"Flies?"

"Of course. Mosquitoes. Gnats. I got a moth last week—he was fluttering around just where you're standing."

"A moth?"

54

"It's the boy's blazer, I think—pure wool, probably. Our friend grabbed some tasty fibres, and on his way out he got a bit too close to the glass. Things got sticky."

"What, you caught him?"

"He was careless. Didn't take basic precautions, and suddenly he'd joined what I think of as a very exclusive club. You want to meet Mr Moth? Come on—he's in the confessional."

"He's still alive? You said it was last week."

"Ah, he'll be with us a while yet. He's preparing for eternity, Spider, and that can't be rushed."

The dog padded to the edge of the wardrobe and stretched his nose up to inspect the particular corner where Thread was now sitting. It took a moment for his eyes to adjust, for all he could see was dust and the mess of another web. Then he realized that there was a curious order to everything. The spider had walkways and even tunnels. The webs were of different densities, and some were sagging with lumpy cocoons.

Thread moved behind a curtain and reappeared beside a large knot of tightly wound silk. The spider lifted a leg and pushed it, setting the whole thing rocking gently. Then it revolved it, and a tiny, wizened face appeared, peering from the end of the bundle. Spider could make out shining eyes, but the head was skull-like and the mouth was a little round circle of distress. Two thin antennae emerged from the forehead, waving weakly, and Spider whined. He could see the creature's shoulders, and beneath them he saw the pale ivory wings which had been compressed and bound tight. The bonds went round and round, intricately tied until the body was encased in a solid, sticky duvet. As he watched, the moth did his best to break free—Spider could feel him straining with every atom of his remaining strength—but the only thing that moved was the mouth, which opened wider and uttered one soft word, so faint he could hardly hear it: "Please…"

"What's that?" asked Thread. "Oh my, did I hear a cry for help?"

"He said 'please'," said Spider.

"They all say that."

"Please!" said the moth again. "Either let me go, sir… or…"

"Or what? What are my options, bug? List them for me."

"Just eat me."

"Why?"

"Kill me! Get it over with…"

"Oh, come on," said Thread, and it chuckled again. "Come now, mister. I thought you had more stamina. We've got things to talk about, as well you know. Your therapy's hardly started—"

"Thread," said Spider. "Stop this."

"What?"

"This is cruel."

"Oh no, this is necessary. Don't talk to me about cruelty, friend—there's no gain without pain. This little chap here, he's got an opportunity to think about his life and realize how insignificant he is. How many creatures get that chance?"

"He's a prisoner. He's suffering!"

"Aren't we all? You've forgotten something, Spider, which is the fact that he came to me. Deep down, he *wanted* this."

"I don't think so," said Spider. "He flew into the web because he didn't see it—because you built it as a trap. That's what you do, and it's called a trick. I think you should let him go."

"Then what do I eat? Are you going to share your dog food?"

"Yes!"

"No. Anyway, he'll thank me in the end—they always do.

What I give these guys is *time*, and they're not used to it. They get time to reflect on the dumb decisions they've made, and their stupid, miserable relationships. 'I was so happy!' they say, and I help them to see that happiness for what it was. An illusion, buddy—because the suffering starts as soon as you're born."

Thread swung the cocoon round and set it rocking.

"You understand that, moth?" he cried. "Of course you don't—not yet, but... Spider? Where are you going?"

"I'm getting down."

"Why?"

"Because I don't like it and I don't think it's right."

"Oh, wait!" sighed the moth. "Don't leave me!"

"Spider," said Thread. "We haven't talked about you yet—and your own crisis. When are we going to do that?"

"Never. I don't *want* this."

"No? That's because you're in denial, friend. You don't know what you are or where you're going, and neither does the boy. Life is work and pain, and then you're dead!"

"I don't believe you!"

"You think you're happy? Look at you."

Spider had had enough. Before Thread could speak again, he jumped wildly down, crashing hard on to Tom's desk. A mug of pens and pencils overturned, and the dog skidded as they rolled beneath his paws. He spun, and his tail caught the computer screen, tipping it over the edge. Spider heard the crack, but there was nothing he could do. He leapt to the floor and nosed his way swiftly out of Tom's bedroom and down the stairs.

Phil was on the landing, and he patted his head. His hands smelt of fish food, so Spider made a bolt for the kitchen, where he found his own bowl. He swallowed a biscuit and took himself out into the garden. At last he could shake himself and drink in the fresh air.

The moth's face wouldn't leave him, and those sad words, "Don't leave me!", were still ringing in his brain. He shook himself. There was nothing he could do, and to think about misery only made him miserable.

Spider noticed a ball on the grass and picked it up in his jaws. Then, for a horrible moment, he saw himself as Moonlight had seen him: a mindless dog, with a plastic toy in his mouth. What did he want with a grubby white ball? Did he want to bounce it and chase it and wear himself out? Yes, was the answer. Yes. Was that really such a crime?

A door slammed in the house, and he turned. It was later than he thought! There were running feet, hammering down the hall. Then came the cry he'd come to know so well, and he found himself spinning and barking as he tripped over his own paws. It was Tom's voice, loud and excited.

"Spider? Spider!"

He was overwhelmed by instinct. He dropped the ball and belted back into the house, sliding over the kitchen tiles. His master was there, having dropped his bag and his blazer. They launched themselves at each other, and Tom caught him, spinning to the floor, as usual, in a somersault of tangled legs.

"Spider!" cried Tom. "New game, OK? You're a sniffer dog! Come on—get me! Catch me!"

It was a different kind of chase, and Spider caught on at once. He grabbed at Tom's arm as Tom thrust it out, retreating up the hallway. Tom pushed him off with a shriek and made his escape, his shirtsleeve tearing as the telephone rang. Up the stairs they ran, and after a quick wrestle on the landing, Tom announced that by some miracle he had no homework, so it was time for the park.

They played until dusk, then watched TV. Phil cooked supper, and when Tom took Spider upstairs the rain fell gently, pattering on the skylight that wouldn't close.

The boy slept under the duvet, with the dog curled up on top. They turned and squirmed, and the phone rang again in Tom's dream—on and on, until he cried out, trying to answer it. Spider licked his hand and felt the fingers stroke his muzzle. They played over his tooth and finally lay still.

I'm a guard dog, Spider thought happily. Then he thought of Moonlight again. *Unless somewhere—somehow—I'm a cat.*

8

Tom discovered the broken monitor the very next morning.

It was a real problem because it meant he couldn't print his history project, and that was due the following day. He'd been working on it for three arduous weeks, researching and writing, but without a working screen he couldn't even save the files and transfer them. He was totally stuck.

"And how did it break?" asked his dad.

"It fell off the desk."

"Fell off the desk? You mean you dropped it?"

"No."

"So it jumped off?"

"I think maybe, possibly... Spider could have knocked it."

His dad was exhausted. His shift had changed again, so his sleep pattern had been turned inside out. He was trying so hard not to be irritable, but he stared at the dog and shook his head. Spider looked at the carpet.

"Don't let him into your room," he said slowly—and when Tom went to reply he just held up his hand. "I'm not arguing with you. That animal's costing us a fortune. Have you any idea what we still owe for the van? For the damaged cars?"

"No."

"No. You haven't ever asked."

"I'm sorry, Dad, but he's still settling down. He's doing his best."

"Aren't we all? Just don't expect me to pay for a new computer, OK? You can do without."

Tom was dreading his next history lesson.

It was lesson three, just before break, and it started well. Instead of gathering in the homework, the teacher seemed keen to show the final section of a DVD, which was to be the climax of the module. By five past eleven, the Nazis had stormed across most of Europe, and seemed unstoppable. The bell would ring at exactly quarter past, and when it rang Tom would be safe: he wouldn't have to hand anything in until the following Monday. By next Monday, he would have begged or borrowed a monitor and sorted the problem.

He waited with his eyes closed, counting down. With two minutes to go, he sensed the classroom lights flickering, and the German army was ominously still. Dr Vokes had pressed the pause button.

"Good," he said. "So now we understand the true horror of Nazi aggression. What, Kasia?"

A girl in the front had her hand up, and Tom knew what she was about to say. He could see a fat bundle of papers on her desk, and her eyes shone with enthusiasm.

"Do you want our projects in, sir?" she asked. "They're due today, aren't they?"

There was a groan, which the teacher silenced with a glare.

Tom sat rigid and still.

"Thank you," said Dr Vokes. "I should have collected them at the start of the lesson, but we just have time—thank you for reminding me. Hand them in now, please—pass them along."

There was an immediate rustling. Twenty-three children produced their projects, each one neatly bound according to the rules.

Tom didn't move, and his desk was idiotically bare. His mind was whirling, and his stomach churned: should he hand in an old bunch of notes, and buy himself time? Should he put his hand up and confess, or say he'd forgotten? In a dither of uncertainty, he simply went red.

Dr Vokes turned, as if he'd sensed the boy's discomfort, and looked straight at him. The sun caught the lenses of his glasses, and all Tom could see were two pitiless discs of light.

"Thomas," he said.

"Sir."

"Your project, please. Aparna, can you start gathering them in? Make sure your names are on the top sheet—you've had ages. Tom, get on with it!"

"Sir, yes. I was going to talk to you."

"You're talking to me now."

"I mean, at the end of the class."

"Oh."

"Yes."

"We don't need a conversation. I just need your homework."

"That's the thing, sir—I had a bit of a problem. At the last minute."

The room was horribly silent. Aparna was taking in the folders, but quietly, and every boy and girl felt the warm stirrings of dread and excitement. Tom, the victim, was looking only at his hands.

"Oh dear," said Dr Vokes. "Three weeks to get it done. The deadline repeated every lesson and noted in your diary... and you have a problem on the very last day. How unfortunate."

"Could I have an extension, sir?"

"No. I'd like the work now, please."

"Could I hand it in tomorrow, before registration?"

"No. I'd like it now."

Tom said nothing.

"Where is it?"

"At home, sir."

"Why?"

"I had a problem with my... computer."

He'd said the wrong thing, and he knew it. Dr Vokes hated technology, priding himself on the good old-fashioned fountain pen. The bell sounded, shrill and long—but nobody moved, and nobody wanted to. Everyone was watching, for the fuse was burning and the explosion was now inevitable. The teacher was ominously still, and even though the corridor outside was full of running feet and laughter, the silence in the room was unbreakable. Nobody twitched, for everyone was savouring the scent of pure, undiluted fear.

"Look at you," said Dr Vokes quietly. "What is a boy like you doing at a school like this? Stand up."

Tom stood up.

"Two demerits. Detention on Thursday. And I'll speak to your tutor. Oh, and wait... Look at me."

Tom looked up.

"Why are you such a mess? Look at your shirt."

"Sir?"

"How often do you change it?"

"I don't know, sir."

"Don't you?"

"No, sir."

"It's grey with filth and it's torn. It's your only one, isn't it?"

Someone sniggered.

"You're a disgrace, boy. Have a word with your mother and tell her to buy a new washing machine. When you find me tomorrow, at eight o'clock sharp, I want you to be clean. I don't want an urchin from the slums: I want someone with a bit of self-respect, who's visited a barber and learnt how to dress. Now get out!"

Tom stared, too upset to move.

The teacher had turned pink, and his spiteful mouth contracted into a sneer of loathing. "Get out!" he roared. "Go! Now! Leave!"

Tom was swirled through the doorway with the other children, and found that he was running. The last thing he wanted was an encounter with the other boys—especially Robert Tayler—so he ducked to the right and then the left, past the sixth-form centre, and into the library.

He didn't stop because he still wasn't safe. He needed the reference section, at the far end: that was where the librarian had her office, so that's where he went, grabbing the nearest book and plunging into a chair. It didn't matter what the book was because he couldn't have read the words even if he'd wanted to. He just stared at the pages, his hands shaking, as he wondered what to do. He thought of Spider, waiting for him at home, and that was the only thing that calmed him down. Three more lessons and a lunch break: he could endure them because afterwards he'd be with his friend, and they'd be back in the park. They'd go for a walk, farther than ever before—right up on to the heath perhaps, where they could be lost and alone. His breathing eased, but the tears in his eyes stayed there, quivering on his eyelashes.

"You all right, Tom?" said a voice.

It was Mrs Mourna, the librarian. He hadn't seen her, but she'd seen him arrive and was looking straight at him.

"Yes, miss."

"What's that you're studying?"

"Oh, it's... just something I found."

"How's your dad?"

Tom blinked back the tears.

"He's fine, miss, thank you. Working hard."

"Good. You'd tell me, wouldn't you, if something was wrong?"

"Yes, miss. Thank you."

The librarian was beside him, crouching low.

"How are you settling in?" she asked. "The first year's always the hardest. Are you enjoying school?"

Tom nodded desperately. He was holding his breath because he knew he was about to shatter. His eyes were burning, so he kept them open wide and they just stayed dry.

"It's great," he said, and managed a laugh. "Thanks, miss—I'm loving it."

9

Meanwhile, Spider couldn't settle.

Perhaps he could feel Tom's anxiety from afar, for he'd been up to the boy's room several times and stood there, wondering what to do. Phil was downstairs, so he had the run of the house still. He checked the garden and sat in the kitchen, but he felt trapped and uncomfortable. He thought about the little moth and shook himself out from nose to tail: there was no point dwelling on problems he couldn't solve—and he didn't want to think about Moonlight. He crept back up to the bedroom, and that was when he heard Phil.

"Spider? Come on, boy..."

He was calling softly in case he woke Tom's father. Spider

could hear him moving about downstairs, and it sounded as if he was in a hurry. The back door opened and closed again, and Spider trotted on to the landing. The front door was open too, and he was about to investigate when he heard Phil pull it quietly closed. There was a scrape of metal, then, as the moped was hauled off its stand. The engine started, and Spider couldn't believe his good fortune. He listened as the bike puttered away into the distance.

Spider had the run of the house again.

He did a quick tour to check he was really alone. Tom's dad had his door closed, so he padded past that and went back downstairs. He wasn't hungry, but it always made sense to see if there was food available, and he could smell the tantalizing scent of digestive biscuits. He found the packet, open in the lounge, and though he knew it was wrong, it was all too easy to reach up and bring them down. It was even easier to crunch and swallow them, and when the sugar exploded in his system he felt a burst of energy that sent him racing back up to the landing. As he did so, he noticed the door to Phil's room: it was ajar, leaking the usual mix of engine oil and deodorant. Spider had never set a paw over the threshold, and wasn't quite sure he dared.

He put his nose in and looked around the walls.

Every bit of space was covered in pictures of motorbikes. There were beer bottles and at least half a dozen ashtrays, which made the air rather sour. He was about to retreat when he saw a flicker of movement, like the flaring of a match. It was a bright orange flash, and it came from a bowl in the corner.

"Hello?" said Spider quietly.

The bowl was perfectly round, and full of water. He put his nose to the glass.

"Oh, wow," said a voice. "How are you?"

It was Hilda the goldfish, and she was swimming in a circle. She was moving slowly, keeping close to the side, and the voice had a bubbly quality: small and friendly.

"Fine," said Spider. "Thank you."

"All OK?"

The fish completed a circuit, and bobbed for a moment, staring from wide eyes.

"Good, thanks," said the dog.

He stepped closer, and the fish set off in the opposite direction.

"How are you?" asked Spider.

"Oh, I'm good too," said the fish. "Thank you for asking. Quite a day, though, huh?"

"I suppose it is. I haven't actually been in here before—this is new to me."

"Really? Why do you say that?"

The fish paused. She flicked her tail and set off on another circuit.

"Because it's true," said Spider. "I'm thinking that I ought to go upstairs and wait for Tom. This isn't my... territory. I mean, Phil seems like a nice person, but I don't know him as well as I do my master, so I ought not to intrude. I wouldn't normally be indoors like this."

"Why do you say that?"

"What?"

"Huh?"

"Why do I say that? Because it's true. I'm usually in the garden. I'm not sure Tom's father likes me, and... Well, he makes the rules."

"Why do you say that?"

Spider paused. "Why do I say what? Which bit?"

"Huh?"

"What?"

"How are you?"

"Look," said Spider. "I'm fine, but I'm just trying to work things out. I've caused a few problems, to be honest. I always worry a bit, because I wasn't chosen—you know, in the beginning. I was the last dog and they couldn't sell me, what with this tooth. I'm not much to look at—that's obvious—so when Tom's dad saw me, I was given to him. I was a free gift, if you like—I had no value. That doesn't bother me now, but it's something I have to remember when I'm thinking about how I fit into the family because, well, the family's a strange one, when you think about it. There's something going on that I don't really get, but I love Tom, and he loves me. I love him to bits, but his dad wanted a cat, which I completely understand. Cats are… very attractive. They're easy to care for, and they don't cause the kind of problems I do. Maybe I should try to be more catlike."

"Hmm," said the fish. She twirled in a circle and blew a bubble. "Why do you say that?"

"Because it's true. I know about cats. I know one cat in particular, and I keep thinking about her. She said some very strange things."

"Huh?"

"She said I might have a cat's soul."

"Wow."

"I know. But what does that actually mean? I can't work it out, but if she's right, then I should be with her. You're a fish, aren't you, so I don't suppose you have these problems…"

"Oh, no. You bet."

"Well, then. If you know what you are, you do what you do. You do fish-things in the same way as I do dog-things. Maybe."

"Why do you say that?"

"Look, I'm trying to explain… I'm just trying to make sense of it all. Fish swim and eat and… that's how it should be. I'm looking at you, and I can see that you behave in a fishlike way. What bothers me is that I'm still not totally sure what I am, because—"

"Why do you say that?"

Spider barked with frustration. "I'm explaining!" he cried. "I'm thinking it through! How can we know what we are? I love Tom, but he's not a dog. He's human! He throws sticks, and I catch them and bring them back. He's doing what he does, so I do it too, and we all get along."

"Why do you say that?"

"Oh, you're not listening!"

"Huh?"

"This is hopeless—you're just repeating the same dumb question. I'm talking to a fish—why am I even doing that? You don't communicate with your owner, do you? Phil, I mean. Does he love you? Maybe he does, in a way. But I sleep at the bottom of Tom's bed, and in the night if I wake up and feel alone, I realize I'm not. I can feel his heart. I hear it. I'm serious. Just listen—don't speak. Have you ever found that your heart is beating in the exact same rhythm as someone else's? That's what happens with us. Tom smells of me, and I smell of him. But what I'm trying to work out is whether there's more, and… Oh dear, what if Moonlight is right? Tom might change, and what happens then? Thread, too—I haven't told you about Thread. It thinks things are going to end badly, so I'm living in a kind of constant fear. Not all the time—I don't mean that. Most of the time I *don't* think—I just get on and live my life, but… you only get one, Hilda. You don't want to ruin it, and I saw how big the world was. I was on the roof and I saw it, spreading out for miles."

The fish bulged her eyes slightly, and blew a trail of bubbles.

"It's so, so big," said Spider softly. "And you think I'm a mixed-up fool, I know you do."

"Huh?"

"I've got to stop thinking. This is way too deep."

"Hi."

"What?"

"Why do you say that?"

Spider howled in anguish, and butted the fishbowl hard with his nose. There was a crack, as loud as a gunshot, and the water slopped out over the table. The dog watched in horror, for the bowl had split and the fish was flicking her tail in alarm. She did two quick circuits, bubbling anxiously. She tried to do a third, but got caught in the weed, which marooned her on a handful of damp gravel. She flopped on to her side, gasping, for the water had run on to the carpet.

"Oh no," whimpered Spider.

"What?" said the fish quietly.

"I'm so sorry…"

"Why?… Why did you do that?"

Spider gazed at the destruction, feeling more helpless than he'd ever felt. The fish was still opening and closing her mouth, but there were no more words.

Spider fled. He raced downstairs and straight back up again. He rushed into Tom's room, diving on to the bed and burying himself in the duvet. He was shaking all over, aghast at what he'd done, for the dreadful thing was that there was nothing he could do to put it right. He squirmed back on to the floor and jumped up on to the table. Pens and pencils went skittering in every direction, and he caught one in his mouth and bit hard. Then he was on the floor again, snapping and biting. For five mad minutes he pulled at everything he saw. There was a slipper with a loose sole: it took him ten seconds to rip it apart. There were action figures, and he hurled them into the air. Tom had board games that he never tidied away, and Spider upended them, tearing the boxes. The cuddly dragon came next, and then he attacked a cushion. The air was soon thick with feathers, and the carpet was invisible under a chaos of ripped fabric. There was the felt penguin Tom kept under his pillow. There were the roller skates that stank of leather. There was the golf club, cold against his teeth, and the box of comics that flapped and flew. It soon looked as if the whole room had exploded. The wardrobe was empty of clothes, and Spider was rolling in the mess he'd made. He remembered Moonlight's magical claws, and tried out his own on a pair of training shoes. He went down low, like a cat and hunted them, and then he returned to the felt penguin, shaking it so hard it fell apart.

By mid-afternoon he'd transformed Tom's bedroom into a mass of fluff, feathers and ripped-up paper. There were places to roll and tunnel, and, best of all, the whole nest had the intoxicating scent of himself and his master combined. He lay there, panting in relief—and that was when he noticed Thread, dangling just below the skylight.

The spider was smiling.

"My word," it said. "What a dog."

Spider stared.

"What a lovely mess you've made. Are you happy now?"

"Yes. I think Tom's going to be surprised, but—"

"Pleased?"

"I think the whole place looks better than it did. Don't you?"

Thread descended, and once again Spider heard its thin, cruel laugh.

"I think he'll be overwhelmed," said Thread. "I can't wait to see his reaction, because you've really done it now. For sure."

He paused, for they could both hear the front door opening, and weary feet in the hall.

10

Spider jumped off the bed, his ears flapping.

The feet came slowly up the stairs, treading heavily. They paused on the landing below, and Spider remembered the goldfish. He had a vision of the broken bowl and the water as it flooded the carpet. He heard Tom's voice, then, but it was quieter than usual.

"Oh, no," said the boy.

Spider padded to the door, and was in time to see Tom as he reached the bottom of the staircase. The two friends looked at each other.

"Spider," said Tom, "what have you done?"

Spider sat down.

"Why are you in the house?" the boy asked, and he started up the stairs.

Spider wagged his tail once and lifted a paw. He could sense a terrible fatigue in his master, and he knew that things were about to go horribly wrong again.

The boy was close now, and he had a bewildered look. His tie was twisted, and there was mud on his blazer. When he put his hand out to touch Spider's head, the back was grazed and bloody. Spider whined and licked at it, but Tom was moving past him, into his bedroom. He stopped and stood motionless, as if some magic wand had touched his shoulder and turned him to stone.

"No," he said softly. "Oh no, Spider. What the hell have you done?"

The dog watched in alarm as Tom gazed around his bedroom, shocked and upset. The boy sat down suddenly on the carpet—it was as if his legs had given way. He put his face in his hands, so Spider did the obvious thing and bounded into his arms, nuzzling hard. He was pushed away, so he pushed back harder, more frightened than ever. He squirmed between the boy's elbows, whimpering, and tried to get a good lick at the troubled face—and he saw, with horror, that the face was bruised, and the right eye swollen. Tom turned his back and rolled over on his side.

"No!" he said—and he said it again and again. "No. No. No."

Spider whined, hunting for a solution. He thought of the stick game—could that make things better? The closest thing to hand was a wooden ruler, which he'd tested his teeth on earlier and rejected because it splintered so quickly. He found its remains in a mess of feathers and brought them over to his master, pushing at the boy's chest.

Tom looked at the gift and got unsteadily to his feet.

"Spider," he said, "you're a bad dog. Do you understand me?"

Spider didn't.

"Look at this mess. Look at what you've done... This is..."

Tom was lost for words. He stared at the wreckage around him, and picked his way through the debris, to what was left of the felt penguin. It had been decapitated, so he looked harder and soon he found the head. The beak was missing.

Spider got ready, still wondering if things really were as bad as they seemed. Was Tom tricking him? Maybe he would throw the penguin and everything would be all right.

Tom didn't. He looked at it and said, "Why? Why today? As if I haven't had enough. Oh..."

The boy gulped and closed his eyes.

"Do you know how long I've had this?" He held the remains of the toy in both hands. "Spider, this is Penny. But you don't know that, do you? This was the first thing I was ever given, but you don't understand that, do you?"

Tom's voice was doing strange things, and Spider whined again.

"This was the first thing I ever had, as a baby. Mum made me this. She made it, and said... She said..."

Tom paused and shook his head. Spider saw the tears running down his face. His whine was constant now, for he realized things were even more out of control than he'd thought. It felt like the world was ending.

"You can whine all you want," whispered Tom. "Whine away..."

Spider yelped.

"Just look at that—that's my English book... That *was* my

English book, and that *was* my French dictionary! Jesus, Spider—you've ruined them all. This is a disaster... It's over."

He put his hands over his head, and moaned.

"Dad's going to kill you. And me. We might as well run away together because we're dead, both of us. You're a bad dog! D'you hear me, Spider? You're a bad dog. You've learnt nothing. You're... you're a monster."

With that, Tom turned away and left the room.

"Nice one," said Thread.

Spider didn't answer. He stood there, unable to comprehend the tide of misery that had rolled through the bedroom. He hadn't understood Tom's long sentences, of course, but he'd heard the words "kill" and "bad dog". Worst of all was the total rejection of every lick and nuzzle: he'd been pushed away not once or twice—and not as in a game—but every single time. Every effort he'd made had failed, as if Tom had become a stranger. The relationship was over, just as Moonlight had predicted.

"What do I do?" he said faintly.

"Don't ask me," said the spider. "All I know is that you've blown it. For ever."

"Don't say that, Thread. I need advice!"

"You need to face facts. The kid's a worse mess than we thought. You just saw it yourself. He's hot, then he's cold. He has no stability, does he? He's emotionally wrecked. That's the problem here: one minute he's all over you, and the next he's blubbing over a toy penguin his mummy gave him. He called you names, dog."

"That's not fair—"

"Of course it's not!"

"I mean, what you said isn't fair. I've let him down again!"

"What I said is *true*, dog. And, no, life isn't fair. What do you want, you stupid mutt? He insulted you and he threatened you."

"I need to say sorry."

"What for? For being what you are?"

"No! For spoiling things!"

"How's that going to work? 'Sorry, master, I've been behaving like a dog, because that's what I am.' He's psychotic, that kid—and violent, too. Did you see the blood on his hands?"

"He was hurt."

"He's a bully!"

'No! I think he's in trouble, and I've made it worse—"

"Oh, Spider, come on! He's got friends at that crazy school, and they've been fooling about together, fighting. The one thing he doesn't need now is a pet like you. He's tired of you, didn't you see that? And it's so, so typical. This is how relationships go, every time—and it proves what I've always said. Stay single—if you have any guts you'll get out now. Listen… Shh! Wait."

Thread and Spider felt the vibrations together.

"Someone's coming, dog—and it doesn't sound good."

"What do I do?"

"Attack."

"Attack who?"

"Everyone. It's the best option, buddy—always is."

The feet were heavy on the stairs—heavier than Tom's. Spider whined and moved backwards. When he saw who it was, he started to shake. It was Tom's dad, and it looked as if he'd just got out of bed. He came into the room and surveyed the wreckage in silence. Then he picked up the plastic sole of a wrecked sandal. He slapped it against his palm.

"My God," he said. "You've ruined us."

Spider was silent.

"They told me you had a bit of retriever in you. Retrievers don't do this, do they? What the hell's going on? What are you? Come here—come on..."

Spider tried to retreat, but he was trapped between the bed and the wall.

"Bite him!" hissed Thread.

Spider shook his head.

"Go on, get him!" cried the spider. "Go for the throat!"

But things happened way too fast for that. Tom's dad lunged forward and caught Spider by the collar. He was yanked off his feet, and though he twisted like an eel he couldn't resist the man's strength and determination. Half strangled, he was dragged out of the room and down the stairs, bumping on his back. He yelped and barked, but the collar was twisted harder, and all he could do was screech. Then he heard Tom. The boy was screaming too, and his dad was yelling at him.

As they crossed the landing, Spider did his best to howl. Tom ran at his father, but was pushed back. He came again, grabbing at his dad's arm—and that was when Spider's instincts kicked in. He bit hard at the fingers that held him, but he couldn't get purchase, and he was lifted off his feet again. He struggled and snarled, but suddenly he was in the kitchen, the door shut and locked behind him. Tom was hammering at it, and Spider felt a rush of cold air as he was hauled into the garden. His windpipe was completely blocked now, and he knew he'd pass out if he didn't get free. He twisted wildly, slashing with the claws of his back feet. Then he saw the shed, upside down, and he found himself flying into the furthest corner.

"I've had enough!" cried the man.

The door slammed, and Spider lay in the darkness. He heard footsteps retreating, as Tom's voice cried out from the house. It was silenced abruptly, and there was a terrible stillness.

"Ouch," said someone.

Spider blinked. He couldn't even whimper, for he was concentrating on breathing. He didn't think anything was broken, but he wasn't sure he could stand. He licked his muzzle and shook his head slowly, trying to clear it. Then he rolled over and managed to look around him. He could just make out a window, but it was nailed shut, and the whole place felt small and claustrophobic. There was no way out.

11

"Are you all right?"

Still, Spider said nothing. He was too shocked to think, and his ribs were aching. He waited, and his heartbeat gradually slowed so he was able to swallow.

"Look, don't worry," said the voice. It was a tiny, nervous sound coming from a corner of the roof, soft and whispery. "If you're moving in, that's fine—I won't be in your way. You can hardly see me—and I'm not here to cause trouble."

There was silence again.

"You're hurt, aren't you?"

"No," said Spider.

"You ought to stay still for a while. You might have a

concussion, or something, so... I'd take it easy if I were you. What's your name?"

Spider went to speak, but the words wouldn't come.

"Don't worry," said the voice. "I'm only a moth—we don't need to communicate if you don't want to. I like dogs, though—always have."

The creature laughed, and it was a soft, fluttering sound.

"'Only a moth'," it said. "Ha! I don't mean I'm ashamed of that. I just mean, well... you know, that's what I am. I stay out of the way, so if you're going to be here for a while we can live together without any kind of, you know, territorial problems. I'm busy, and I mind my own business. I just, you know, try to get by, doing my thing. Where are you from?"

Spider had managed to stand, and he limped to the door. He snuffled at the gap beneath it and listened hard. There was no sound or scent of Tom's dad, but he was still trembling.

"I've been here most of my life," said the moth. "A lonely old life, in some ways. I was never that sociable, till I met my partner. That was late in life, really—but that's often the way. You don't find happiness till you've given up looking. That's when it drops in, out of nowhere."

The moth laughed. "We're inseparable now, and we've got this shed just the way we want it. You'll be a welcome guest. Am I talking too much?"

"No."

"Good. I can be a chatterbox, especially when I'm worried."

Spider felt wings fluttering past his left ear, and spied a grey shape hovering above his head. He closed his eyes.

"You're from the big house, aren't you?" said the moth.

"Yes. I think I've been thrown out, though."

"That's too bad."

"I can't stay here. This is… a disaster."

"Can I just quickly ask you something?" said the moth. "While I've got the chance."

Spider nodded.

"It may not be the right time, because I can see you're upset. But I have to enquire: have you ever been up to the top bedroom? There's only one, and it's way up in the roof. You get in through a broken skylight."

Spider nodded again. "I used to live there," he said.

"You know it well? Oh, good! You haven't seen another moth up there, have you? One like me. Because my partner, the moth I was telling you about… He was looking around up there with a view to relocation. He'd found something rather special in the wardrobe—a jacket of some kind, made of wool. He brought me a few threads, and it was top quality. He's been gone longer than usual, though, and, well, to tell you the truth, he's never been gone this long before, and I can't help thinking the worst."

Spider said nothing.

"He's a skinny old thing," said the moth. "Smaller than me, and a kind of off-white. Delicate features. Not young, not any more, but… handsome in his way."

"I haven't seen anyone," said Spider.

"Oh, well. You'd know him if you saw him—his eyes are pale and prominent. Magnetic, really. He's not talkative, though—not like me. I just need to be patient, I think. Sit it out, eh? What else can you do? When you love someone, you wait for ever—you're incomplete without them." The moth laughed again. "He'll be back with some stories, I imagine. But I just wish he'd, you know, contact me. He may have met someone younger, for all I know—I've never been much of a looker, but we were a pair. We had something special, I'd say, but I don't think I ever told him just how special he was. Maybe I did, but it feels so strange when it's just me, and I keep thinking I hear his wings, and I... I need to see him. I want to tell him that I need him."

"What's that noise?" asked Spider.

"I don't know. Where?"

"Above us."

The moth listened. "Oh, that's not him. That's just a cat. I can hear shouting again, too, in the house. There's a hole up here, and you can see the whole garden. Yes, there are quite a few by the look of it. I can see tails."

"What colour?"

"Hard to say. Black, I think."

Spider pressed his nose to the crack under the door and breathed in. The scent wafted down to him, and was unmistakable. He felt faint all over again.

"Moonlight?" he whispered. "Moonlight, is that you?"

Silence. Then he heard the sound of claws picking their way over the shed roof. Something jumped down, and he heard a snigger, which was cut off by an abrupt "Shh!"

"Moonlight?" hissed Spider.

"Yes."

"Moonlight, you have to help me."

"Oh," said the cat softly. "Is that really you? Darling, how badly are you hurt?"

"I'm fine. I'm locked up, though. Listen, this might be the end, if you don't help me. It's a long story, but—"

"I saw it all. I was watching you—didn't you see me?"

"No. When?"

"I've been watching you all afternoon. I was up there, on the roof again. Oh, you've forgotten me!"

"No, that's not fair—don't say that, Moonlight. I've just had the strangest day, and I'm so confused. I can't seem to do the right thing, ever. I've been bad..."

"That's not true. What can you be, other than yourself? I saw you tearing the little boy's room to pieces. You were so brave!"

"I wasn't. And I've killed a fish!"

"That's good!"

"It wasn't—she was harmless."

"Oh, they pretend to be, but they're slippery creatures. You're wild at heart, you see, Spider—I so wanted to be with you."

"I'm being punished now. I don't know what came over me, because I shouldn't have been so... so destructive. They'll send me away."

"Where to?"

"I don't know. The dogs' home, possibly. I need to get out of this shed. Look for a latch, will you? If you can see the bolt you might be able to pull it."

"If only I could. I just haven't the strength, Spider."

"I'm sure you have, if you try."

"No, no—you must break down the door. If that wicked man returns, or the boy, they'll have no mercy. I can still hear them, shouting like savages! Do you think they want to kill you?"

"I don't know! Tom wouldn't hurt me—"

"Oh, but he would—and you must hurry! Free yourself, Spider, before it's too late. If I weren't so feeble I'd tear down the door myself! You should be running with cats, not languishing in jail."

Moonlight's voice lifted to an agonized wail, and Spider felt the fur on his back rise up, so that he shuddered all over. Another cry soared up in response, and the air was full of frenzied yowling. Spider turned in his panic, and kicked at the wall. It held firm and fast, but he felt weakness in one of the slats. He spun around and attacked it with his nose.

"Hurry, Spider!" cried Moonlight. "You're right—you're not safe in there."

He pushed harder, and felt splinters pierce his flesh. A gap appeared, though, and he thrust a paw right through it. There was a whole chorus of cats now, shrieking together. Inspired by their screams, Spider got his teeth on to an edge and crunched.

"So close!" hissed Moonlight. "Come to me, Spider! Chase me!"

Spider closed his ears, for the sound around him was torture. He kicked and chewed—and suddenly the wood twisted and gave way. He had a hole big enough for his head, and by driving hard and ignoring the cuts and scratches, he got halfway out.

"Moonlight," he cried. "Use your claws! Help me!"

"Oh, you're like Samson!" purred Moonlight, retreating. "Push, Spider. Fight for love!"

"I can't fight for anything. I'm stuck."

"No!"

"Dammit, it's my collar. The collar's caught—can you lift it?"

"No, Spider—my paws are too soft."

"I can pull back if you support me. Wait! It's coming—I can feel it!"

Spider turned himself upside down and kicked with his back legs. His collar had been stretched already, and the frayed leather could take the strain no more: it snapped apart, and he was free. Another slat splintered around a rotten knot, and he could almost taste freedom. He lunged forward, ignoring the pain, and rolled on to his belly in the mud.

That's when he heard the noises from the house. The back door had sprung open, and a torch beam was dancing down the garden, sharp as a searchlight. It flashed straight into his eyes, and for a moment blinded him.

"Spider!" cried Tom.

"We're lost!" hissed Moonlight. "He's after us, and what have we done? Run, my angel!"

"Where to?" asked Spider.

"I don't know!" said Moonlight. "Oh, the world's not big enough!"

He heard Tom's voice again, shrill and desperate: "Spider! Stay!"

There were footsteps racing over the grass, and he saw a flash of silver as Moonlight disappeared under the fence with the other cats. Spider leapt sideways, and the light hit him again.

Tom's father was shouting, too, but it was the boy's voice that screamed loudest: "Spider! Don't go!"

The dog spun round, torn in two. He saw the boy's wild, panic-stricken eyes, but at that very moment Moonlight shrieked, and the dog obeyed his instincts: he scrambled into an alleyway and dashed after her. The cold air gave him the energy surge he needed, and he was running faster than he'd ever run. Tom was calling him still, but his voice was fading. His friend was above him, and Spider was a pet no more. He felt a rush of terrifying, dizzying independence, and he pounded through another garden, and through its gate. The cat was still ahead of him, and he bounded after her with his ears closed. He had no idea where he was going, but he was free.

Tom called Spider's name until he was hoarse.

At last, a long howl of anguish ended in a sob, which was swallowed by the night.

He listened for a bark, but there was nothing, so he stood by the fence, trying to comprehend the disaster.

His dog was gone, and he was alone.

PART TWO

Jesse was a fox.

She was two years old, and a rich, coppery red. Her current home was the Denham Estate, but this was only a temporary lodging. She'd found a network of well-made tunnels there, and they were safe, warm and comfortable. But, restless by nature, she knew that she'd be moving on soon. Why stay in one place when the world was so vast? Change was not just inevitable, but exciting—and Jesse always liked to observe new creatures. This was why she'd become interested in the newcomer: a black and white dog who appeared to be called Spider.

Was he someone's pet? Clearly not. He had a skinny, hungry look and always seemed anxious. On the other hand, he wasn't vicious or wild, and he didn't have the manic energy of a stray. What confused Jesse the most, however, was the company the poor creature kept. He spent most of his time with a gang of cats, who Jesse had come to loathe. She could see a couple of them now, padding about by the bins beside the main kitchen, so she moved further down the slope and took cover in a rhododendron. The dog crossed the lawn to join his friends. It was obvious he was starving.

Moonlight was worried, too.

Denham Manor was one of a dozen homes she considered hers, and it was probably the nicest. It was certainly the furthest from town, and perfect for the occasional weekend when she needed to relax. There were three other cats, who adored her, and she had thought it would be rather fun to present Spider to them. He'd been such an easy conquest.

Things were getting complicated, though, and she sat in the drawing room with Lady Denham, wondering what to do next. The old lady was frail and feeble. Two full-time maids looked after her, and they both had strict instructions to give Moonlight anything she wanted. One yowl in the kitchen produced not just milk, but warm milk, and there was always a bowl of something edible. Monday had been braised liver, while Tuesday had been a little too rich—some kind of spiced chicken she would have preferred to eat raw. Today, however, had been a triumph: a mixed-fish dish without a single bone, choice flesh in a creamy white sauce. The cat had overeaten, and now felt fat. When she eased herself on to the old woman's lap, she had to work hard not to be sick. She purred, and felt gentle fingers behind her ears.

"So," said Lady Denham quietly. "Who's been a naughty girl, eh? Who's been staying away and getting up to mischief?"

Moonlight yawned.

Lady Denham was a bore. The cat suspected she was dying, for she often passed out on the sofa with the TV blaring, and there was always drool around her mouth. Moonlight gazed at her now, wondering if she'd make it through another winter. Her death would be so inconvenient, for the manor was comfort of the traditional kind, and she didn't want to lose it.

"So then," said the old woman. "Who's that nasty old dog?"

Moonlight arched her back, and forced herself to perform a gratitude rub—she had a whole routine of appropriate responses, and they rarely failed. She would close her eyes and stretch. She'd open them again, and butt gently with her forehead. She rolled sideways sometimes, waving her paws as if helpless. These three moves could make Lady Denham coo like a child. Nine times out of ten it would result in a sweet, as it did now: a cream puff that she didn't really want, but couldn't reject. She licked at the cream, surprised that the old woman had even noticed Spider.

"Is he your little friend?" she said.

No, thought Moonlight. *You couldn't call him that.*

"He's your little friend, isn't he? What are we going to do with him?"

Moonlight was just asking herself the same question. She knew she ought to go to check on him, to be sure he was still there, and not doing something foolish. That meant going out into the cold, where the other cats were waiting, and she was losing interest in the whole silly game. She'd tricked several dogs in her time, but they'd mostly been strays who'd soon given up and moved on. Spider seemed to have an unusual loyalty, and she didn't know what to do with it.

"You should bring him round to the kitchen," said Lady Denham. "Feed him up a bit, no?"

No, thought Moonlight. *The kitchen's mine.*

She jumped down on to the carpet. Lady Denham called her back, so she showed her backside and walked briskly into the hall. The mirrors told her she was still beautiful: there was one up ahead, so she practised her purposeful stride. There was one to the right as well, so she checked her whole aerodynamic form, adjusting her tail and lifting her hips. She could hear a servant clattering about, so she pushed through into the boot room, where a flap let her out on to the terrace. There, she breathed in the scent of hyacinths for a moment, before moving on to the pond. Spider would be waiting by the sheds and bins. That was where he slept, and she saw him at once, standing awkwardly. He was wasting away, and his fur looked awful.

"What kept you?" he asked.

"Oh, darling," said Moonlight. "Don't start."

"I'm just so hungry. Did you find anything?"

"Nothing."

"Nothing at all?"

"They're so mean. I tried and tried—I begged. What could I do?"

"I don't know. Can dogs eat potatoes? There's a store round the back, but I don't know if I can digest them, and they're covered in earth."

"Spider, you must try. Have you checked the bins?"

"Twice. I found something in a packet, but it's disgusting. It made me feel ill, Moonlight."

"What, darling? Show me. Beggars can't be choosers, you know."

"I think it's rotten."

Spider picked up a crushed cardboard box. There was a picture on the front, and even though it was torn and stained with old tea leaves, the image was clear enough. A smiling woman was spooning a meaty substance into a bowl. All that remained of the dish was a smear of brown, glutinous goo where the packet had been opened and emptied. Spider dropped it in disgust.

"It's a McKinley's Pet Snack," said Moonlight. "She buys them for me, but I can't eat them."

"It smells terrible," said Spider. "You haven't caught anything, have you? Anything fresh, I mean?"

"Not a thing. Oh, this is torture! They won't have you in the house, angel. I've told them straight: 'He's not what you think! He may look like an unloved, scavenging mongrel, but look deeper. He's a cat at heart—or he could be.'"

"I'm getting thin."

"Yes, darling. You wanted that, didn't you?"

"No. *You* wanted that. I don't think I should lose any more weight. It's making me feel faint, and…"

Moonlight shook her head. "Have you been climbing? That's what you need to do, Spider. Doesn't he, Butter? Butter, darling, tell him what he needs to do. He's so stubborn…"

Another cat had appeared on the shed roof. This one was a youngster, with a damaged ear. She had no access to the house, but lived comfortably in one of the abandoned cottages. Hughie was just behind her, with Pigeon. These two lived with one of the servants. They knew their place, keeping to the shadows and standing by to assist Moonlight should she need them.

"Dog," said Butter, "Moonlight is absolutely right: you should practise your climbing. It's essential for survival."

"You must listen to us," said Pigeon.

"I am," said Spider. "I've done what I can, but I'm facing facts now—or trying to. I'm just not much of a climber."

"Oh, sweetheart!" cried Moonlight. "Give up now, and it's all been for nothing. Don't do that to us. We've come so far together, and here you are among those who love you most. Look, tomorrow we'll break in and get you a proper meal."

"But you said that days ago," said Spider. "It's been half a week, maybe more—"

"I do what I can!" cried Moonlight.

"I'm sure you do, but I'm so hungry."

"You want to leave me—I can sense it."

"That's not what I'm saying."

"Leave, if you must."

"But where would I go? Where's the town, Moonlight? I've no idea where I am."

"Just follow your heart!"

"Listen," said Hughie suddenly. "What about a nice, fat squirrel? They can be quite tasty, if you don't mind gristle. They're nutritious, too."

Moonlight turned to him. "That's a wonderful idea, Hughie. Why didn't you mention it before?"

"I thought you'd seen them. There are loads, up in the cedars."

"I can't remember everything, can I?" said Moonlight. "I can't take responsibility for every little thing."

"Of course not."

"We thought you didn't like rodent," said Pigeon.

"It's not for me!" hissed Moonlight in frustration. "Sometimes we have to think about others and *their* needs. Now, where exactly are they? Which tree?"

"Just over the bridge. There are some old ones who can't run very fast, so they wouldn't be hard to catch. We could get one now—I'm sure we could."

"Spider, this is your chance," said Moonlight. "A real hunt!"

"It would be fun," said Hughie, and he leapt up on to one of the bins. "They're easy to kill, squirrels. I remember when you caught that baby one, Moonlight—you kept it alive all day!"

"He tried to scratch me."

Hughie nodded. "That's true. You bit his legs off in revenge. He was no match for you."

"Small creatures never are," said Butter.

"I don't know," said Moonlight. "Sometimes I think my killing days are over. Isn't there too much conflict in the world already? Why can't we just love one another, and live in peace? That was one of the many things that drew me to Spider: he's kind, you see, not cruel. And who wants blood on their paws?"

"I agree," said Pigeon. "Let's forget it."

"Forget what?"

"The squirrel."

"No, Pigeon—how can we?" said Moonlight. "If Spider is to learn real independence, he has to develop key skills. In any case, squirrels are filthy animals. They deserve to die."

2

The group moved off together, and the fox followed at a distance.

The cats padded through a gate on to the second lawn, and went towards the largest of the ponds, over an ornamental bridge. The trees beyond were huge, spreading their branches low. They sat down around Spider, so Jesse checked she was still downwind, and crept a little closer. Soon, she was within earshot—and the cats were so engrossed in their conversation they didn't look round.

"It's not simply about claws, Spider," said Moonlight. "It's about determination."

The other cats were nodding.

"I understand that," replied the dog. "I'm sure determination is very important, but in the end I just can't grip. We can't pretend otherwise—mine aren't long enough."

"Aren't they?" said Pigeon. "Let me see."

"They're not sharp, either."

Pigeon sniffed at one of Spider's paws.

"Hmm," she said. "They are rather blunt."

"Oh, darling, do try," said Moonlight. "Try for me, and I'm sure you'll succeed. Butter, why don't you go first, and guide him?"

"Very well," said Butter, leaping on to a branch. "The first bit's easy, so watch and learn."

"It may be easy for you," said Spider.

"A kitten could do it."

Spider gritted his teeth and put his paws up on the trunk. There was no way he could heave himself upwards, and he could feel the cats' impatience.

"I can't do this," he said.

"Then look over there!" cried Moonlight. She pointed with her chin. "Look at that long bough, and how it sweeps down to the ground. Come round this side, Spider—you're in luck. Even you can get on to that."

Everyone moved together, and Spider saw that it might be possible. A great clump of foliage had weighed one of the lower branches right down, so Spider jumped and scrambled, and managed to get himself on to it. It swayed under him, and he went down on his haunches. He was trembling already, but that may have been from weakness.

Moonlight, meanwhile, drew herself swiftly up the central trunk, and was soon poised prettily above him, looking down. The other cats joined her, keeping a respectful distance.

"Come on, mongrel," said Hughie. "Come towards us."

"Hughie, angel, don't call him that," said Moonlight. She looked at Spider.

"You're doing marvellously. Try and straighten your legs—and always look up."

"Never look down," said Pigeon.

"Use your tail," said Butter. "Get it up."

For Spider, it was like being back on the roof, when he made his perilous journey along the ridge. He didn't dare straighten anything: the only way he could make progress was to cling to the limb and inch along it using his elbows. Every lump and bump had to be dealt with slowly: a twig in the wrong place meant careful manoeuvring, and a new cluster of foliage was a nightmare, because he had to close his eyes to butt through it. He still had splinters in his shoulder from when he'd broken through the chicken shed: now they were joined by countless shards of hard, spiteful bark that were forcing their way into his muzzle.

"Try jumping," said Moonlight, and Spider just managed to suppress a growl of frustration.

Eventually, he reached the main trunk, and saw it was a good four metres above the ground. His head was spinning. At least it was obvious what the next move had to be: another bough reared upwards, just above his ears, and he could see that where it divided, there was a series of branches that interlocked, like stairs. The cats had realized this too, for they had all moved together and were arranged over them.

"You've done the hard bit, doggie," said Pigeon.

"Where's the squirrel?" asked Spider.

"At the top, I'm afraid."

"They always hide up there, the rotters."

"Cowards."

Spider sighed. "Look," he said. "Wouldn't it be more sensible if you went and found them? I don't think I can get much higher, and even if I can—"

"Don't say that!" cried Moonlight.

"Why not?"

"Because self-doubt is the most wicked enemy, darling. You must vanquish it through bold aspiration."

"No. Moonlight, please. I don't know what words like that even mean, but this clearly isn't working."

"*Try*, Spider!"

"I have been!"

"Then do it for love! Faith is what you need to give you wings—and if you die in the attempt, so be it! At least you will have burned brightly, like Icarus. Keep going, angel! Help him, Hughie!"

Hughie jumped down and skipped the next few steps as an example. The others mewed their encouragement, and the dog realized he had no choice.

Spider put both ears back, and launched himself wildly at the next branch. His paws made contact with something solid, and he swung there, scrabbling. Before he dropped backwards, he pushed again, heaving himself upwards. He grabbed at leaves with his mouth, and when his tail got jammed, he hauled it free, whimpering under his breath. Suddenly, he was in the centre of the tree, wedged in a V-shaped branch he could wrap between his forepaws. He hugged it, waiting to be sick. The whole world was swaying wildly.

"Oh, Spider!" cried Moonlight. "You're so funny! Look at him..."

The dog closed his eyes. He was panting again and shivering all over. His ears were full of dirt, and he'd got a mouthful of ants, which were scurrying around his gums—he could feel several exploring the back of his throat. His left nostril was cut, and he had blood all down his chin. He blinked, and the tears cleared his vision: Moonlight was looking down, with her head on one side. She eased herself gracefully along a branch and dropped on to one a little lower. Tail high, she poured herself down, and padded daintily towards him.

"You're a warrior," she whispered. "Will you chase me for ever? Don't speak! Rest now, for you're halfway there."

Spider groaned. "I think I'm finished."

"In what way, brave heart?"

"I've come as far as I can, and I've lost another life—maybe two. I'm not a cat, and I don't want to be, and... Oh, where's the wretched squirrel?"

Moonlight turned and looked upwards into the leaves.

"Where's the nest, Pigeon? Can you see it?"

"It's empty," said Pigeon.

"Oh."

"I think they probably heard us coming," said Butter. "Our friend was just a little bit noisy, I'm afraid, so I think they've moved on. Unless we've got the wrong tree."

"Bother," said Moonlight. "Run up and check, would you? It seems a shame to give up now."

"I'm at the top," cried Hughie. "Butter's right: they've scarpered."

A breeze stirred the leaves, and Spider coughed.

"Is anyone cold?" asked Pigeon. "How are you, Moonlight? It's late for you, isn't it?"

"Oh, don't worry about me," said Moonlight.

"You mustn't get sick," said Butter. "You should be indoors."

"I know—that's just what the vet said, when he was speaking to the old woman. 'Don't take risks', he said—and here I am, reckless as ever. Love is so, so dangerous."

She cleaned a paw and looked at Spider.

"Let's think," she said. "It might be best if you stayed here till the morning. If you're quiet, the squirrels may come back, and then you'll be able to get one for breakfast. You'll be safe enough, won't you?"

"Where?"

"Here."

"No," said Spider.

"Why not?"

"Because I'm halfway up a tree, Moonlight. I'll freeze, and then I'll fall."

"But I'm looking at it logically. When the squirrels come back, you'll be perfectly placed, and—"

"Moonlight, no. How can I stay up here? Just look at me."

The cat came closer and looked at the dog's hunched, twisted form.

"Darling, you may be right. All I want is what's best for you, so I think *you* should make the decision. I have to go, obviously, but if you want to abandon all this, and go back to that little boy... well, perhaps you should."

"Moonlight, I'm lost."

"Aren't we all? Perhaps that's the only thing we ever know for sure."

Spider felt his head swim.

The breeze blew harder, and the tree leant sickeningly as the branches groaned. Spider was losing his footing, and the ants in his throat were making him cough. Pushing up with his right leg, a piece of bark came away, and he nearly slipped. Moonlight stared at him, and Spider managed to grab the branch between his chin and his chest."Don't leave me," he said quietly.

"I think I must," said Moonlight. "I will kiss you, though, because a kiss will keep you warm all night."

"I don't want a kiss!"

"No?"

"No."

"We did our best, didn't we? I won't forget you, Spider, and I feel that you won't forget me, so—"

"Moonlight," said Pigeon, "I'm sorry to interrupt, but—"

"Wait, please. I'm saying goodbye to a very special dog. He's tried so hard, so hush for a moment. We're all beginning to realize that we can go no further as a team, and our experiment has failed."

"We've got a visitor, Moonlight—"

"Pigeon, please!"

"She's right under us."

"Shh!"

Moonlight put a paw on Spider's shoulder and closed her eyes. She pushed her nose towards the dog's forehead, and was just about to lick him when his hind legs slipped again. His body swung sideways, and all he could do was kick wildly. He launched himself upwards again, and his skull smacked hard into Moonlight's. The blow sent her spinning backwards, legs flailing. Spider yelped in horror, and found he was tumbling after her.

Neither animal had time to cry, though Butter, Pigeon and Hughie all shrieked in alarm. There was no real danger to Moonlight, of course, for the cat was used to jumping, and her feet were ready for the grass. Unfortunately, Spider landed directly on top of her, and while that cushioned his own fall, Moonlight had the air driven from her lungs, as she was squashed face first into a knotty root. The dog rolled to one side, and lay stunned.

That was when Jesse saw her chance—and took it. Spider glimpsed a blur of fiery red, and caught a powerful smell as she attacked. The fox's jaws closed on Moonlight's neck, and shook her like a rag. The bell on her collar tinkled wildly, and she tried to free herself, clawing the air. Jesse tossed her high, and prepared to catch her again for the final crunch. How the cat escaped death, Spider would never know.

Moonlight turned a complete somersault and somehow swivelled in mid-air. She wasn't quite quick enough, though: Jesse got her again, but only by the tail. She swung her round, the cat slashing madly. She twisted, so Jesse hauled her round the other way, in two dizzying circles. The cat leapt for her life, as the fox bit harder. The next moment, the tail was in two pieces, and Spider saw Moonlight's mutilated backside disappear across the lawn. He tried to chase her—but she was gone, and all that remained was a glimmering trail of blood.

Jesse spat the furry remains into the grass and looked at the dog.

"Close," she said, licking her lips.

She grinned, then, and laughed a rich, throaty laugh.

Spider could hardly move. He stared at the tail stump, and tried to find words: they simply wouldn't come.

"Don't tell me you were friends," said the fox.

Spider blinked. "We were," he said weakly.

"Well, I'm sorry, in that case. But she was asking for it. Why is a dog like you hanging around with trash like that? What's your name?"

"Spider."

"You're in a bad way, Spider, old chap. You need food and shelter, and a good night's sleep. What are you sniffing at? What's wrong?"

Spider blinked and looked up.

"It's her collar," he said quietly. "She was proud of that."

"Ah, forget it."

"This is awful, though. Will she die, do you think?"

The fox barked. "What's she going to die of?"

"She's been hurt! Look…"

"Ah, it's only a flesh wound, Spider. She'll be back soon, more's the pity. You haven't seen the last of her."

"Then perhaps I should look after her tail. We could mend it somehow. Reattach it, or—"

"No, we couldn't."

"No?"

"Spider," said the fox, "are you telling me that you were genuinely fond of that animal? Because if so, you're weak in the head. She was playing with you!"

"She liked me. I felt sort of drawn to her. She was…"

"What?"

"Oh, it's hard to explain. She was so confident. She said I might be half cat, you see, so—"

"Half *starved* is what you are," said Jesse. "What you need is meat, because you're not functioning, friend—that's probably why you're saying such ridiculous things. Leave the tail, and leave the collar. Come on—I'll look after you."

"I don't think I've ever been this lost," said Spider.

The two animals had been underground for at least twenty minutes, and the dog was exhausted.

Jesse paused, and waited for him to catch his breath.

"It's a side tunnel, this one," she said. "It connects up with the main drag, and brings us to the heart of the den. You know what a den is?"

"A kind of home."

"Well, this is all part of mine—and you're welcome to it. Nothing safer than a tunnel…"

Spider couldn't see a lot, but his eyes were slowly adjusting. He could make out the walls, which were rough earth, and he knew they'd been trotting downhill for quite some time. One passage had led to another, and then Jesse seemed to double back. There was a smell of fresh, clean air and Spider found himself in a well-ventilated chamber covered in soft, dry leaves.

"What do you think?" asked the fox.

"Nice."

"I didn't build it, but I like to think I've made a few improvements. For one thing, we have a larder now. How do you feel about pheasant? Killed her yesterday, and there's still enough for two."

"I think I could eat anything," said Spider.

"You settle down to that, then. There's a spring nearby, so once you're done we'll go for a drink. I'm off tomorrow—don't know where yet. Just keen to see new places, I suppose. You're from the town?"

Spider nodded. "I was."

"Welcome to the country. What made you leave your home?"

Spider sighed, and told him the whole story. The fox busied herself by dividing up the bird. She made sure her guest got several rich, tender pieces of breast meat, and the dog was soon chewing with an overwhelming sense of relief. Food had never tasted so good, and he could feel a trickle of energy slowly returning.

"Thank you," he said, at last.

"I'm happy to help."

"Do you always share like this?"

"No. But I've been on the run more than once, and I know about hunger."

Spider nodded again, and the fox sat down.

"So you had a master," she said. "What was his name?"

"Tom."

"Was he a youngster?"

Spider nodded.

"And you felt you had to leave? You just had to get out?"

"I don't know now," said Spider. "I can't get the sequence straight in my head, but Moonlight said Tom was coming to kill me—and he *was* shouting. His dad's pretty fierce, and I just panicked, Jesse. There was a torch in my eyes, so I was half blinded."

"Sounds bad."

"I was thinking about Thread as well. He said it would all end badly, and he was absolutely right."

"And Thread is?…"

"A spider."

"A spider? You don't listen to spiders, surely?"

"I listen to everyone. I'm not that clever, you see, and Thread said I was in what he called 'an unsustainable relationship'—"

"Hang on," interrupted Jesse. "What does that even mean?"

"A friendship that can't go on."

"Why couldn't it?"

"Because I was bad."

"How, Spider? What did you do?"

"Oh, I went crazy. I tore up some of his things, you see—including his penguin."

"You killed a penguin?" gasped the fox. "Where was this?"

"In his room."

"Tom kept a penguin in his room?"

"Oh, no—it wasn't a real one. It was a toy, but Tom was devastated. He said…"

Spider hesitated, and looked down.

"What?" asked Jesse.

"This is awful. Tom said it was the first toy he'd ever been given. By his mother."

"Can she get him another one?"

"She's not around, Jesse. And this is a secret, but I know he dreams about her. I've heard him, and… Something's going on, and I don't know what it is, but she calls him on the phone, or tries to. Every day."

"That's tough."

"He won't speak to her. I dream about my mother sometimes, but Tom cries in the night, and… It's another thing we had in common."

"Then you need to get back to him, Spider. He disciplined you, and by the sound of it he was within his rights. We all need discipline."

"That's true."

"He sounds like a good, sweet, sensible boy."

Spider whined. "He is! But there's another thing I didn't mention. The dad never wanted me, and I've cost them a lot of money by damaging things, and when I wrecked the room… Well, that was the last straw."

"So they punished you. I'm sorry, Spider, but you should have stuck it out—you know you should. Forget the dad: your master is your master. I've met a few dogs in my time and they never know how lucky they are, because they just don't appreciate what they've got. Between me and you, I get so jealous."

"Why? Jealous of what?"

The fox looked behind her and checked one of the tunnels.

"This is all confidential, I hope? I can speak frankly?"

"Please do."

"Well…"

"What?"

"It's just that, unlike you, I've never been owned. Not by anyone."

"That's because you're a fox. People don't own foxes, Jesse—they don't want them around."

"You're right."

"I'm sorry, I didn't mean to be rude."

"Oh, don't be silly—you can say it. It's a well-known fact, and there's no use disputing it: we're a nuisance. We're seen as vermin, and I can understand that. That's why I've always wondered what it's like to be needed and looked after. It's a special relationship, I imagine. You were together at night?"

"Every night," said Spider.

"You protected each other, then?"

"Of course. We were… inseparable. And I shouldn't have run away."

"Ah, but we follow our instincts—what else can we do?"

"I don't know. I just wanted to get away, out of shame. You know what shame is?"

"Spider, of course I do! We all get it wrong sometimes. I'll give you an example. Let's get that drink, by the way. Are you finished here?"

"Yes. Thank you."

"Follow me."

Jesse led the way through a side tunnel Spider hadn't noticed. It brought them up quickly, and they were back out in the woods. The air was cold, but fresh, and the nearby spring was foaming merrily. The two animals paddled and drank, and then Jesse jumped up on to a shelf of rock. Spider followed, and they rested again, shoulder to shoulder.

"You're asking about shame," said the fox quietly. "Well, I don't know what it is about me, but shame follows me wherever I go. I seem to go crazy, like I'm addicted to bad behaviour."

"Like me."

"Oh no. A lot worse than you."

"What do you do?"

"The other day—I haven't told anyone this, all right?—I was visiting a farm. It's a place I'd been before, several times—you can usually find a snack of some kind, but on this particular occasion the chickens were out. Maybe the farmer had forgotten them, or there'd been some kind of mix-up—I don't know. You never know the background. What I knew for sure was that these chickens were usually locked up, safe and snug, so when you're faced with a temptation like that—well, it's hard to keep control. Are you with me?"

Spider nodded. "Did you kill one?"

"I couldn't resist."

Jesse shook her head and laughed.

"I broke into that coop, Spider, and all the chickens started clucking around, trying to hide. I thought, *Come on, Jesse: do the business. Choose the one you want, and get back home.* There was this fat old bird in the corner, and I didn't think she could move too quickly, so she was the obvious target, and I dealt with her. Fast."

"When you say 'dealt with her', do you mean...?"

"Bit her head off? Yes. And, obviously, I should have left it there."

"Left the head?"

"No, left the coop. I should have taken the one bird and nipped off back to the den, and I don't know why I didn't. It's habit, I suppose—, or compulsion. I'm a fox, Spider—I'm not a philosopher. What I do know is that I couldn't leave, because that taste of blood is... intoxicating."

"Is it?"

"Oh, boy..." groaned Jesse. "It's the smell of it, too—it brings you to a kind of heightened awareness. It's like time slows down, and the colours are unreal—so are the sounds—and you feel so powerful. I went through that place and I killed every single one of them. There were eggs, so I broke them. Chicks? I ripped them to pieces, and once you've started, on you go. You don't want witnesses, for one thing... you don't want to leave the job half done. And the screaming, Spider! Wow, it's like the end of the world."

"Did you really kill them all?"

"I couldn't stop myself. I ended up dragging them out of their stalls, and... oh, some of them were begging for their lives. 'Why are you doing this? Let's talk! Take me, and leave the youngsters!' I was berserk, I suppose—no mercy. The whole place was raining feathers, and there was blood everywhere. I was soaked. I was sliding about, dripping in guts. I ended up back at the den, and this is the thing, Spider: I hadn't brought a single one of those poor birds back with me. I wasn't even hungry. So what does that make me? Did I do that just for fun?"

Spider sighed. "I don't know. Did you get into trouble?"

"No. Of course not."

"You got away with it?"

"I have done, so far."

"But you wouldn't do it again, would you? You've learnt your lesson?"

"I don't learn anything, ever. It's my nature, I suppose. I'd try not to do it again, but if I saw a bunch of chickens and the fences

113

were down, then I'd be in there like a shot. I'd be a fool not to, and… Spider, it's going to end badly, isn't it?"

"What is?"

"Blood leads to blood. That's what my mother said, and it's fox law, I imagine. One of these days I'll meet a nasty end, too. What I need, Spider—what I *want*—is someone like your Tom. A good, kind boy to say 'Hey. Stop that. Bad idea! Stop what you're doing.'"

Jesse whined softly.

"What I need," she said, "is for someone to take me to the park and throw sticks."

"Tom did that for me."

"I bet he did. Did you pick them up?"

Spider nodded.

"Wow," said Jesse. "I would so love to just pick up a stick and return it. Can you think of anything more satisfying? It's such a simple statement of affection. True togetherness."

She paused, and shook her head.

"What?" asked Spider.

"Would I give it back, though? The stick, I mean. I'm not sure I'd be able to."

The dog said nothing.

The fox moved a little closer, so they were warming each other.

"Tom was hurt," whispered Spider. "I think someone had attacked him."

"Who?"

"Another boy. He had a bruised face, as if he'd been in a fight. He wears this red and black jacket, and the pocket was ripped—so was his shirt. I know he's lonely, too, and I told you how he cries in his sleep."

114

Jesse frowned. "That's bad," she said. "It sounds to me as if the boy needs protection. That's what you can give him, so you shouldn't be here."

"You're right, because…"

"What?"

"It's just occurred to me, Jesse. I don't know what I am, but what if I've got a bit of rescue dog inside me? What if I'm part rescue dog? Because if I am, I won't be there for him, which would be the worst thing in the world."

He stood up and yelped.

"How did I end up so far away?" he said quietly. "How did I get everything so wrong? I shouldn't be in the countryside. I'm not wild, like you. I should be in town, with my master, in his bedroom right now!"

"So go back to him."

"But I'm lost. How do I get back? I don't know the way!"

Jesse turned and nipped him gently on the ear.

"Look," she said. "There's no need to panic. You stay the night here, OK? What you need is a good night's sleep—"

"How can I find him, though?"

"I'll help you. We'll set off as soon as it's light. Which town is it?"

"I don't know. There are so many roads and railways."

"We'll find it together."

"Really?"

"Really. It may be a long way, Spider, but we'll find that boy and look after him."

Spider realized that his tail was wagging. It hadn't wagged for so long that it made his back feel strange, and he barked.

"Do you mean that?" he asked. "You'll help me get home?"

"I'd like to meet this boy," said Jesse. "I could come into your garden, couldn't I, and take a look?"

"Of course."

"What would he think of me?"

"Oh, Jesse, he'd love you! I know he would. You're... you're beautiful."

The fox snorted. "Oh, come on," she said.

"No, you're perfect."

"My nose is too pointed, and—"

"It's just right."

"I'm way too amber. Foxes should be a ruddy brown, not this garish red—"

"You're my favourite colour, honestly—Tom's too, I bet."

"Oh. Thank you."

Jesse found that her eyes were full of tears. She nuzzled Spider, and Spider gently returned the nip.

"Tomorrow," said the fox, "we'll sort this out together. First thing."

4

That night Spider had a nightmare.

He dropped into the deepest sleep he'd ever known, and dreamt about a tree-climbing chicken, which was chasing a cat on a moped that ran straight into a spider's web. Tom appeared suddenly, with a bloody face, and Spider woke at once with a bark of fury. He stood, snarling, and saw that he'd been deserted: he was all alone.

When he rushed anxiously up into the open air, Jesse was waiting for him with another pheasant, and Spider ate his portion gratefully.

"Red and black," said Jesse.

Spider looked at her. "What about it?"

"You said Tom wears red and black clothes. I've been thinking about that, and I've seen those colours in a town near here—it's a kind of uniform."

"Yes," said Spider. "It's for school. He has to look smart."

"I've seen people wearing that stuff, and there were lots of them. It's right where the railway goes—"

"Then you've been to his school!"

"I must have been close," said the fox.

"How far is it?" said Spider, leaping to his feet. "Could you take me there?"

"Of course. It's quite a trek, but the sun's shining. We can keep to open country, and find the railway after dark. Then we just follow the tracks."

"Perfect."

Spider put his ears back and realized he was happy.

"Do you know something?" he said. "You're a true friend."

The fox butted him. "Oh, come on! Don't thank me yet. We've still got to get there."

"But you're coming with me? All the way?"

"Try stopping me."

The two animals set off immediately.

Jesse trotted steadily, refusing to let Spider run. They moved together, side by side, and in a short while, they were climbing a gentle hill. They crossed two streams and refreshed themselves, hiding briefly when a jogger came by. By mid-morning the sun was hot overhead and the trees had given way to broad fields. They headed across a meadow, the landscape spreading into the distance under a clear blue sky.

"This is the most direct route," said Jesse. "But we're close to that chicken house I told you about, so it might be better to make a detour."

"You don't want to go there?"

"No. I want to change."

Spider nipped the fox gently on the ear again, and they played for a moment.

"Jesse," he said, as they changed direction. "Can I ask you a personal question? Would you describe yourself as cunning?"

"No."

"Foxes have a reputation for being cunning, though, don't they?"

"I suppose they do," said Jesse. "I've never really thought about it. I mean, I think ahead—of course I do. But cunning suggests playing tricks, and telling lies. I've never told a lie, and I've never played a trick."

"So you're quite straightforward?"

"I hope so."

They came through a hedge, and Jesse stopped. Spider went on ahead, then turned. The fox had scampered to the top of a nearby rise, and had her back to him. One foreleg was raised slightly, and she was still.

"What's the matter?" asked Spider. "Are we lost?"

"No. I might be imagining things, but did you hear a noise just then? What's your hearing like?"

"Good."

"You didn't hear a high-pitched kind of squeak?"

"I don't think so."

"I did. I can hear it right now."

Spider trotted over to his friend, and saw that she had gone absolutely rigid from the tip of her tail to her nose. The fur on her back was standing up, and she was holding her head high, sniffing the breeze. Spider stood close, and realized with a shock that Jesse was nervous.

"What's the matter?" he asked. "Is it an animal?"

"No."

"What then?"

"I don't know. Spider, we might have been a little bit... What's the word? Overconfident."

"How do you mean?"

"We've just cut across open fields, and that wasn't wise."

"Why not? What's wrong?"

"Well, normally, we foxes keep out of sight. That's our instinct, and it's a sensible one because... well, we all know hunting has changed, but you don't go revealing yourself. Can you hear it now?"

"I can hear something, but—"

"It's a horn. I might have to leave you, Spider—I might have to run for it."

"Jesse, you're not making sense."

"I know. I just can't work out which way they're coming. Can you feel something? It's not behind us, is it? This is very, very unlucky."

"Jesse, you're scaring me..."

Spider saw that the fox had turned round again, and that her eyes were bulging with anxiety. He whined, and that's when he felt a tremor in the earth. Jesse swallowed, and now Spider smelt the stink of her fear. There was a fine vibration in the soil, and then, in the distance, they both heard the unmistakable sound of hounds. It was an excited, hungry howling and, rising above it, came the clear, sharp note of a hunting horn. Jesse was paralysed.

"They're not after us, are they?" asked Spider.

The fox managed to blink. "I think they might be," she said. Her voice was a croak.

"Why?"

"Blood leads to blood. I've been spotted."

"Who by?"

"Dear, oh dear. This is suicide."

"Look, if it's just dogs, I can talk to them. I can reason with them—"

"They're not after you, Spider. They're after me, and I know just what they're thinking! They can't believe their luck. We're totally exposed—look at us! And there! There they are. They've got my scent…"

Jesse's eyes were wider than ever now, and she took a pace backwards. She was gazing over the field they'd crossed, to the adjoining woods. A young beagle had emerged from the trees, and it was joined at once by another: both were brown, patched with white. They snuffled the ground, twisting with excitement. A horse appeared behind them, and its rider wore a coat that was blindingly bright—it was vivid scarlet, and seemed to flash in the sunlight. More dogs were appearing, and they all looked up together. They gazed at Jesse, and Jesse gazed at them. For a moment, time stood still.

"What do we do?" hissed Spider.

"I'm dead."

"You can't be."

"This was what Mother said. I don't have a chance."

They watched as the huntsman put the horn back to his lips.

It sounded again, but this time the notes were fierce and urgent. The pack seemed to erupt in movement, for suddenly the whole battalion of hounds was pouring across the field, howling with glee. A dozen more horses crashed through the trees after them.

Jesse had no decision to make now, for there was only one thing she could do: she ran for her life.

Spider saw only the red blur as she skimmed into the next meadow, zigzagging wildly. The dogs came after her, and Spider realized with horror that they were as fast as his friend. He cowered in fear, for within seconds the one in the lead had jumped the hedge he was sheltering under, and the first horse was close behind. The ground was shaking, and he saw vicious hooves churning up the soil as the great beasts leapt over his head. The dogs kept coming, flooding past him in a wild torrent, and he smelt their ecstasy.

"No!" he cried. "Stop!"

They were all the same breed, wide-eyed and joyful. Their ears flapped as they bounded, and they didn't appear to see or hear him. He set off at their heels, running as fast as he could. It was a downhill chase, but he could hardly keep up—his heart was soon hammering in his chest.

Jesse was still out front, and she had gained ground. She was a red speck, pushing into open country, but even Spider could see how dangerous that was. He glimpsed his friend coursing across the land, and saw that the dogs at the front were closer than he'd thought. The fox feinted to the right, and sped off left—but it wasn't a skilful move, and nobody was fooled. In fact, the dogs in the rear were reading Jesse's mind, and could guess where she was heading. With a flurry of barks, they broke from the pack to cut her off from the nearby woodland: it was a pincer movement, and she was certain to be caught. She was forced to cross into another field, and soon the front runners were almost upon her.

Spider pushed himself to the limit, racing faster than he'd ever raced. He put on a final, lung-bursting spurt, and tried to howl.

"Stop!" he cried.

But it was useless. The dogs who heard glanced at him with mad, shining eyes, and he realized with a shock that they were getting stronger as they ran. What could he do? His heart was bursting, but he ignored it, and he suddenly spied hope. A small copse had appeared, and though it was at most only a hundred trees, it meant protection. Jesse flew towards it, gaining ground at last. It was an island of safety, and she shot straight into the thick of it. The front runners hurtled in after her, while those at the rear divided once again, racing round the perimeter to block any exits. Spider saw with relief that the horse riders were stopping at the edge and some were dismounting. The horn sounded a new note, just as urgent and—if anything—triumphant.

There'll be tunnels here, thought Spider, as he pushed into the trees. *There'll be a whole network, like the ones we were in last night. They go on for miles, and she'll be down in one by now. Jesse will be safe!*

"We got a live one!" shouted a young beagle.

"No, you haven't!" said Spider.

"Stay close," said another. "She's not got long, huh? She'll be climbing a tree soon, or trying to..."

The dogs were everywhere, snuffling through the brambles and snorting with excitement. The dreadful thing was that even Spider could detect Jesse's scent, because it was a stink of pure, concentrated terror. He could smell her urine, too, for the copse was full of it, and the dogs were trying to work out where it was strongest.

Suddenly, Spider glimpsed a flash of red. It was deep in the undergrowth, and he whined in frustration. Why was Jesse still visible? Surely she could burrow down and disappear into the earth?

All the dogs had to do was press into the centre. They had formed a tight circle, panting with expectation, and the chilling thing was that they weren't even in a hurry. They were behaving as if the chase was over, and the climax was to be savoured.

Spider tried again. His voice was hoarse, but he called out as best he could.

"Hello?" he cried. "Listen to me, please!"

The pack ignored him, and one dog started to howl.

"That fox is a friend," cried Spider. "Try to understand! You don't know what you're doing. She's a harmless creature, helping a lost puppy."

A large beagle trotted past, wagging his tail.

"OK, boy?" he said.

"No! You have to listen to me!"

"I think we got her this time. We're going in for the kill. Wait for it..."

Spider pushed his way forward, and tried again. "Please!" he howled. "This isn't fair! She's totally outnumbered, and what's the point? Let's just think about this!"

Spider squeezed to the front and turned.

"Look, brothers! Sisters!" he said, panting. "We've all had a fantastic run, haven't we? It's been great exercise, but... listen!"

The dogs were pushing past him.

"Let's show compassion…"

Once again, he smelt the sickening stink of Jesse's fear. The whole pack started to bay, and Spider's cries were lost beneath the noise.

A youngster nipped him affectionately. "You ready?" he asked.

"Please," panted Spider. "Please stop!"

"The real thing, at last. First time for me!"

As he spoke, a couple of the hunters appeared—a man and a woman. They both carried spades, and clambered in among the dogs to hack at the thicket. They were clearing a path to the centre.

Spider howled again out of sheer helplessness, for the whole pack was focused on a cluster of bushes, and red fur was clearly visible as Jesse tried to dig.

"She's gone!" yelped Spider. "She's escaped!"

The dogs didn't hear him—they were so full of joy that they'd closed their ears. They were drinking in the intoxicating scent of the fox's despair. An ominous growling filled the air, for the hunters were nearly through—they were chopping away the last barrier, and the fox was helpless. It was all too obvious: if Jesse were to stand any chance at all, she would have to face the pack and break through it.

Spider howled again, and perhaps his friend heard the cry, for at that moment she leapt for her life and shot towards him. Spider glimpsed her—a red arrow that soared, and then vaulted off a fallen trunk. She rose again, flying upwards over the heads of the astonished dogs. Spider gazed, longing for the miracle that would save her, for what she needed now was a pair of wings. With wings, she could rise higher still and never come down!

Alas, it was not to be. Gravity hauled her back to the earth, and the dogs surged after her. The leader knocked her off balance and a pair of jaws snapped at her tail. Still she might have made it, for she was up again and running. A youngster was just too quick for her, though, and caught her foot in his teeth. She was tripped, and though she tried to turn and attack, the rest of the pack poured over her together, and she disappeared beneath their jaws.

Spider closed his ears, but Jesse's screams drilled through, high-pitched and hopeless, and he glimpsed her just once more. She was there in the centre, for the dogs had her clamped by legs, tail and neck. She was wrenched and torn, and the stink of fear turned to a stench so foul and shocking that Spider found he was open-mouthed, gasping.

He retreated.

He crawled back into the mud, and shut his eyes. It wasn't enough, though: the horror continued till he couldn't breathe, and he had to scurry away into a thicket of brambles, where he curled into a tight, trembling ball. He put his paws over his nose and lay there, panting for breath, until there was silence.

Nobody came for him.

He lay there alone, lost in thought, unable to believe what he'd witnessed, and unable to believe that his new friend had been snuffed out like a candle. The hunt had moved on in triumph, and all he could hear was birdsong—it was as if Jesse had never existed, and he'd imagined the horror. The sun was still shining and the sky was blue.

Spider stood up on shaking legs and tottered on to a footpath. Soon, he came to a lane, which he crossed, and he found himself in long grass. He walked slowly through it, trying to lose himself. The grief inside was so fierce it made him ache, and when he could go no further—when he was more lost and lonely than he'd ever been—he sat down and stared at his paws.

Tom was gone, and now Jesse was gone too—the wise, generous friend who'd saved his life, and listened to all his pain and confusion. How long had he known her? Hardly a day, and she'd been extinguished.

"Blood leads to blood!" she'd said, as if she'd known her days were numbered. And yet she had been looking to the future. She had wanted to meet Tom, and sit in the garden. "That boy needs protection!"—those had been her words, as they'd sat together, shoulder to shoulder.

The sun was sinking, and still Spider sat. He couldn't move.

"That boy needs protection…"

The words buzzed around his ears, and Spider repeated them under his breath.

"Come on," he said, at last. "Stand up, dog. Get up and move! Who's protecting Tom now, Spider? Nobody. And he needs you more than ever, for this world…" He shook his head. "This world is too, too cruel."

Slowly, Spider got back on to his feet, and somehow, despite the aching pain, he managed to walk.

5

That evening, Spider saw himself.

He had no idea how far he'd come, but he arrived at a village and wandered up its main street. He chose a turning at random, which took him between rows of houses. His paws were burning, so he stopped at a lamp post to rest them. Looking up, he noticed a piece of white paper, and there was a photo in the centre. Two faces gazed at him: one was a boy, and he had his arm round a black and white puppy. The puppy had a tooth protruding over its bottom lip, and the boy's eyes were so gentle Spider could only whine. It was Tom, of course, and he had a stick in his hand: his expression of happiness and pride made the dog look away again, for it was too painful. He had no idea who'd taken the picture, or when, and he couldn't begin to understand who might have taped it to this particular post. It had been printed in colour and there were words above and below, with a set of numbers, but as Spider couldn't read, they were a mystery. He noticed that the paper was covered in plastic, which had been carefully sealed at the bottom so it wouldn't get wet.

Spider sat beneath it for a whole hour, as darkness fell.

He wondered where he should spend the night, for he didn't know where the town was—or if he'd been walking towards or away from it. The red and black school had to be somewhere, but where? Tom would be going there tomorrow, probably, and all he wanted was to find him—but how?

He turned down an alley, trying not to think. He stopped by a bin bag which had been split across the middle. Various creatures had explored it already, but he still snuffled about, and managed to find a few damp vegetables.

A bit further on he came to some garages, and beyond them he found a stretch of grass. Nobody was around, so he headed across it towards a duck pond. Three lumps of bread lay at the edge of the water, rejected by the ducks. He crunched them gratefully, and stepped into the shallows to drink.

A sad face looked up at him.

"You're a bad dog," he said quietly. The face looked sadder. "Everywhere you go you cause disaster. Everyone you meet suffers."

Two little girls appeared with a terrier which couldn't stop yapping. They stood under a street lamp, throwing a ball between them, and Spider saw that they were keeping it out of their pet's reach. The dog ran from one child to the other, backwards and forwards, as happy as a dog could be. It wasn't frustrated, or anxious: it just seemed hopeful. The younger of the two dropped the ball, and their pet pounced upon it, snarling with pleasure. Five seconds later, it had given the ball back, and the girls were throwing it between them again. All three were connected: they needed each other, and the game showed no sign of ever ending.

Spider sighed, and took another drink.

A duck had approached, and stared at him with an unblinking right eye.

"I'm looking for a town," said Spider.

The duck said nothing.

"I'm a stranger. Do you know a place where the railway ends? It might be a day's journey or so, but it can't be too far. It has a church, and it's by the sea."

The duck remained silent.

"I'm lost," said Spider. "I've lost all sense of direction, but I need to find this town because I'm looking for a school where the children wear red and black. Black jackets with red on the edges and lions on the pockets—there can't be many places like that. I'm not suggesting you'd know about the school, but does the town sound familiar?"

The duck turned its head and stared out of its left eye.

Spider sighed again. "Maybe you're a stranger too?" he said. "I don't know a lot about ducks. Are you one that flies halfway round the world and always goes in a 'V' shape? Sorry, I don't suppose you speak my language, do you? What I'm saying... It must be just a load of noise, all these meaningless words. Are you wondering about me, though? Are you thinking, *Wow. Why is this dog talking nonsense? Where's he from? Where's he going?*"

The duck gave a short, ugly honk. "You're not a dog," it said.

Spider blinked.

"Are you?" said the duck.

"What do you mean?" asked Spider.

"You're not a dog. You don't look like one, anyway."

"Don't I?"

"That's why I came over. We were talking back there, a whole load of us, wondering what the hell you are. I said I'd go over and check."

"I'm a dog."

"Oh no. Your head's all wrong."

"You mean my tooth?"

"I mean your head. It's the wrong shape."

"How?"

"It's like a cow's head. You're like... What do they call a baby cow?"

"A calf."

"Exactly. I think you're a calf. You've got just the same colouring as a cow, and your head's completely cow-shaped. Why are you pretending to be a dog?"

"Look," said Spider. "I don't know why you're saying all that—"

"Can you make cow noises?"

"No!"

"Why not?"

"Because I'm a dog. If I were a cow, I'd tell you and I'd... I'd give you some milk."

"You can moo, can't you?"

"No."

"Go on, moo-cow. Do a moo."

Spider stood up. "You're joking, aren't you?" he said. "Look at my body: what's all this fur covering my legs? How many furry cows have you seen? And... This is crazy! I thought you were from a foreign country, but I'm realizing now that you're just rude."

"What is he?" said a voice. "Was I right or wrong?"

Spider swung round. A second duck, that looked identical to the first, had approached from behind, and was gazing at him out of its left eye.

"He's a great big fibber," said the first. "He says he's a dog."

"Why?" asked the second.

"Who knows? Maybe he wants to be one."

"He's confused, all right."

"He's sick in the head."

"He's lost it."

"Wow."

The second duck put its beak close to Spider's nose. "My advice, chum, is that you get your scraggy little arse away from our pond—whatever you are. This is a nice area, OK? This is a village green, and the only dogs who come round here come on leads. With their owners."

"That's who I'm looking for!" cried Spider. "I'm looking for my owner."

"So you haven't got one?" asked the first duck.

"Yes, I have!" said Spider.

"Where? You've been abandoned, cow-head! You've been kicked out of the nest, that's for sure. I wonder why!"

Spider was lost for words.

The ducks clucked rudely, and the first one spun round and showed its bottom. It then made the most obscene noise the dog had ever heard—so unpleasant that Spider snapped at its tail feathers.

Both ducks reared up, flapping.

"Protected!" screamed the first, as Spider retreated.

"You monster!" hissed its mate. "We're protected and looked after. We get fed! And what are you? On your own and homeless!"

"Peck his eyes out, Morris! Go!"

They came at him together, honking obscenities. Spider twisted to avoid them, but he was still stabbed hard in the rib-cage—then in a more private place. He rolled over, yelping, and sprinted to the road.

When he looked back, the two ducks were quacking quietly to each other, as they touched wing tips in triumph. Spider limped off, shaken and bruised.

He followed a footpath into the darkness, and at length the track opened out to an allotment. He could go no further. All he wanted was shelter, so he could rest safely and sleep. Thankfully, that's what he found, for there was a shed without a door and he crept into it, curling up at once on an old sack.

He tried to empty his mind of everything except Tom, and he lay there wondering if the boy might come to him in a dream. He remembered his old bed, and how he'd snuggle into the crook of Tom's knees—the boy would stroke him gently, falling asleep as Spider guarded him. Where was he now? What if he'd been persuaded to settle for a cat? What if his father had found him a kitten to love? What if it was on the duvet at that very moment, purring happily as Tom leant down to scratch its simple, undemanding head? Spider closed his eyes and whined.

The dream he wanted didn't come, and the night was a dark one.

6

The sun finally rose.

Spider felt thirsty and sore, and his skin was prickling. Every joint felt stiff.

He shook himself awake, and lifted his leg for a scratch. There was a pinching sensation, as if a needle were being pushed gently into his loin. Twisting himself right round, he managed to get his nose close to the irritation, and, raising his paw higher, he saw the tiniest insect he'd ever seen. It had wormed its way deep into his coat, but he could still make out a greyness. It seemed to have its head jammed out of sight, but even as he watched, the little creature shifted itself around and looked up guiltily. There was a tiny spot of blood on its face, and Spider knew at once that it was his own.

"Sorry," said the creature.

The dog was too astonished to speak. He was looking into pale, watery eyes, and they gazed back at him under a pair of waving antennae. The body was slowly turning pink, and trembling with pleasure.

"I'm topping up," said the little insect apologetically. "We've all got to live, Spider—that's what I say, and I just try to be discreet. In and out, that's me—but this is a sensitive area, I'm aware of that."

The creature crawled a little higher and propelled itself upwards. It jumped high, landing elegantly on Spider's nose. It burrowed forward, into his fur, and stared at him without blinking.

"You're a flea," said Spider.

"I am," said the flea. "Through and through. You mustn't feel badly about it. Sometimes I meet animals who think we're a reflection on their personal hygiene, but that just isn't the case. What I look for is good company, and that fox—bless her—she was as clean as they come."

"You really knew her?"

"Oh, totally. We'd been together for a long time, Spider, and she did her best. You can say what you like about the chickens she killed, but nobody deserves an ending like hers. Nobody."

Spider swallowed, and sat down.

The flea had clearly drunk deep, and was now cleaning its jaws.

"You did everything you could," it said. "You tried to save her, and that was brave."

"Where were you? Did you see the dogs chasing her?"

"I was right on your shoulder. I'd made the changeover shortly before, when you were talking together. I heard the whole story about the little boy, and that's when I transferred to the warmer heart. That's what I do, you see—I'm temperature-sensitive. At least they were quick."

"What were?"

"Jesse's last moments."

"Were they quick? It took a long time, I thought."

"I don't think so. She didn't suffer too much, and she went down fighting. It's hit you hard, friend—I can see that. You had an understanding, and she was an ally. She was right about Tom, too—spot on. You shouldn't have left him, and you know it."

"What's he doing now, I wonder?"

"Looking for you."

"I doubt it. He's probably glad I've gone."

The flea sighed. "You're depressed. You're more lost than you were as well. You need to find that town and sort things out."

"I need to find the school. I'm going to walk in and find Tom."

"It's a good plan. So what we really need is a map, or a road sign."

Spider shook his head. "I can't read. Can you?"

"Not properly. I lived in a library for a while, so I can trace out a few letters, but I'm not saying I'm literate. What I suggest is that we head back the way you came and find an intersection. There'll be a main road somewhere, and you can follow that."

"It's a long way," said the dog. "That's the only thing I'm sure of."

The flea pinched him gently. "Then we ought to get going."

"You said 'we'."

"Why not?"

"You want to come with me?"

"I think we can help each other. We should work together, in honour of old Jesse."

"And your name?"

"I've never had one. I'm not really the social kind—but I'd like to meet Tom."

"That's what Jesse said. Tom would have absolutely loved her. *I* loved her."

"We both did. What you need right now, though, is breakfast. I don't mean to be personal, but your blood's a little bit thin at the moment, and that means low sugar. I'm going to come up on to your ear, OK? And if you need a good scratch, just let me know."

"I've never had a flea before. How irritating are you?"

"I'm pretty discreet. But when you want me to leave, just say the word. I never take it personally."

"OK. Let's go."

The allotment was still quiet.

Spider trotted through it, and it wasn't long before they both spotted a compost heap. Once he'd cleared away some grass cuttings Spider was able to salvage several bacon rinds and the remains of an egg. He washed them down with fresh rainwater, and immediately felt stronger.

There was a faint mist rising around them, and the sky was rosy.

"Did you see the picture on that lamp post?" asked the dog. "It was me and Tom."

"Where?"

"I don't know. Somewhere round here, but I'm confused."

"You and Tom on a lamp post? I must have been fast asleep."

"It was a kind of poster. It had letters and numbers, so if we

137

found that again, maybe you could work out what all the words mean."

"I could try."

"Why haven't I got any sense of direction? I have no idea where it was."

"Don't worry about it. Some dogs have an inner compass, Spider, and some dogs don't. The main thing is to be patient and methodical."

Two hours later, however, they still hadn't found it.

The village had come to life around them, and there were cars making their way slowly out of garages. They passed many poles and posts, but every one was bare, and Spider soon realized he was walking in circles. He couldn't pick up any familiar smells, and the only landmark he really remembered was the duck pond. On the flea's suggestion, they revisited it, and sat at the edge of the grass.

One of the ducks made a rude gesture, and Spider turned his back.

"We were definitely here," said the flea. "You didn't mark your territory, did you? Personal question, I know, but—"

"I wasn't in the mood."

"Sure."

"I was in shock, to be honest. I still am. And we're getting nowhere."

"Ah, you're impatient. You're emotional, too—you keep getting hot. That doesn't help, Spider. I understand your distress, but I suggest we calm ourselves down and work a little more systematically. Now, which side was the pond on when we first saw it?"

"It was on my left."

"Which means you came from up there, by the petrol garage."

"But we've been there, haven't we?"

"No. We've been everywhere else, but we haven't been there. Let's take it slow—there's absolutely no hurry."

Spider tried to keep calm. The flea was now at the tip of his ear, holding tight, so they both had a good view of their surroundings. They crossed the street, and found themselves on the edge of a housing estate.

"Familiar?" asked the flea.

"Yes."

"OK, but slow down. Let's *walk*, OK? What's that coming up on the left? A lamp post."

"It's not the one."

"So keep going, and look at the next lamp post. By the blue car—do you see that one, over on the other side? That's got something attached to it. Now, don't get your hopes up…"

"You've done it!" cried Spider. "It's still there—I can see it!"

The dog could stand it no longer. He dashed across the road and sprinted along the opposite pavement. Sure enough, it was the paper, safe inside its plastic jacket. The tape had come loose, so the top corner was flapping, but there was Tom, smiling down at him, and his left arm was draped around Spider's very own neck. The dog jumped up and rested his paws below it.

The flea crawled forward, and peered at the photograph thoughtfully.

"You really think that's you?"

"Of course it is."

"You're sure? You must have been younger."

"So maybe I've grown. Maybe I've changed, but I'm telling

you: that's me, and that's Tom, and we're in the garden together. I never should have left! Now, what do the words say?"

"Well, there's a whole line of numbers, which could be anything. And the words, well... I'm just spelling them out, so give me a moment. You've got an 'M' for 'mother'. You've got an 'I' for... something else. Then there are some of those snaky ones—what are they?"

"I don't know."

"Two of them, and another something... Then it's another 'M' and another one I've never seen before—some kind of circle."

"So what does it spell?"

"Alphabets are hard. Something beginning with 'M', but..."

"What about 'My'?"

"'My something'? It could be. My guess is that it's someone's name. 'Miss', perhaps. Or some kind of code, or just a pattern. How old is Tom?"

"Eleven."

"Does he like drawing?"

"He loves drawing."

"Could just be decoration, then. Why decorate a photograph, though, and strap it to a lamp post?"

Spider wasn't listening. He had noticed something, and the flea felt his temperature rise again.

"I don't believe it," said the dog.

"What?"

"We're in luck. You've brought me luck, flea. Look over there, on the other side of the road."

Spider whined—he couldn't help himself. Jumping down from the lamp post, he took a few paces forward as the fur rose up along his spine.

"That boy," he said quietly. "I know him."

"Where?"

"Coming out of the house—coming towards us. I recognize him, and look at what he's wearing…"

"He's wearing uniform. He's going to school, and—"

"But look at it! It's red and black, and it's got the gold badge. It's the boy on the bike: his name's Rob."

"A friend of Tom's?"

"I wouldn't say a friend, but he used to come to the park sometimes. What's he doing here?"

"It's where he lives, I imagine—"

"He'll take us to Tom, then, won't he?" yelped Spider. "If we just follow him, he'll lead us to the right place. This is fate! Oh, flea, you've solved the problem!"

"Spider, wait. He's going to think it very strange if a stray dog tags after him. You're sure you know him?"

"It's Robert Tayler, and he goes to the same school!"

Spider was right.

The boy had said goodbye to his mother, and was now moving briskly along the pavement, with a rucksack on his back. Suddenly, he broke into a run and, for a wonderful moment, the dog thought he was coming to greet him. He barked once, but the boy crossed the road and sprinted down the street, raising an arm as he ran. Spider turned and saw what he was chasing: a long, single-decker bus was moving down the street, one light flashing as it eased into a lay-by. Robert was racing towards it.

Spider gave chase at once, tearing over to the opposite pavement. The bus stopped as he got to it, and its doors opened wide for a girl who was in just the same clothing as the boy.

Spider ran round to the back, and saw that the bus was completely packed with children in identical outfits—there were no adults at all. Some were small, and some were big. Most were wearing earphones, staring into space, but one looked up, and seeing Spider, started to wave. Another boy saw him too and grinned. All Spider could think to do was bark. He barked and jumped up into the air, for Tom had to be among them somewhere. He dashed round to the front again, and some of the children were cheering now. He raced to the doors, but they closed against his nose, and the wheels were starting to turn.

The bus pulled away, and Spider's barking turned into a howl of anguish, for what could he do? He gave chase, running down the road as the vehicle gathered speed. The back window was full of heads, laughing and shouting. Hands were waving, but the bus was accelerating all the time, and soon Spider was racing flat out in a mad sprint he couldn't possibly sustain.

Seconds passed, and the houses came to an end. The bus was surging ahead, and the road joined a wider one that bent in a long curve. Another light started to flash, and Spider found himself among hooting traffic. A car skidded around him and he had no choice but to dive to the side. He watched as the bus joined the stream of traffic and disappeared out of sight.

Pawing the ground, he let out a final howl and shook his head in disbelief. There was foam around his mouth and he was trembling.

"Wow," said the flea. "That was quite a ride."

"We lost him."

"We did."

"So close. *So close!* Are you OK?"

"I've been sick, I'm afraid. That was terrifying, Spider. You can't do that to me. I just need a moment... Sorry."

Spider felt the tiniest pinch in his ear, and he waited as the flea drank deep again. He stood up, aware that his paws were on fire.

"Sorry," said the flea at last. "If I'm empty I die."

"You help yourself."

"My word."

"What?"

The flea belched quietly.

"Your blood. It's gone straight to my head. Why don't you sit down? We need to keep calm and take stock."

The flea moved carefully down on to the dog's nose, and the two creatures stared at the road.

"I've had a thought," said Spider.

"Good. Take it easy, please. Step by step."

"I'm trying to be methodical," said Spider. "And I'm remembering something: Tom didn't get a bus in the mornings, so he can't have been on that bus. He walked to school, you see. That means we must have lived close by—close to the school, because he walked to it."

"It makes sense. But who came out here to put the picture up on the lamp post?"

"I don't know. Do you think it's possible that Tom's looking for me?"

"Of course he is, Spider. Why wouldn't he be?"

"Because he was angry! He could be angry still. Perhaps... What if he wants me caught and punished? I mean, what if Jesse was wrong, and Tom hasn't forgiven me? That's what the paper could mean: 'Missing dog! Must be found!'"

"To be punished?"

"To be sent away. To be put in a home for bad dogs."

"No," said the flea. "That doesn't sound like the Tom you've described, Spider, and I don't think you should jump to conclusions.

What we have to do in situations like this is trust our instincts. That means finding the school, which was your first idea. If we're lucky, we'll run straight into your master and we can sort things out. That's the mission, OK? And we keep it simple."

"We should follow the bus, then."

The flea nodded. "Yes. It's shown us the way. But I need to say something now, Spider—and I don't mean any disrespect, because I know you're doing all the work and I'm just a passenger—but you're going to get yourself killed."

"How?"

"You're going to get run over!" said the flea. "You're not as good on the road as you need to be—and I'm worried. I was once on a badger who dashed around like you. He ended up under a truck, and it wasn't pretty. You've got to keep calm, friend. You've got to use your head."

"I just want to find Tom," said Spider softly. "That's all I want, because I should never have left. Even if he hates me now and wants me dead. Even if I've been replaced and forgotten, I want to see him once more—if only to say sorry. I want to lick that hand and say a proper goodbye."

"Sure," said the flea. "That's called loyalty."

"Is it?"

"I've never felt it myself, but I admire it in others."

Spider took a deep breath. He gazed at the cars and lorries heading for the town, and started walking.

7

Tom's day had started well.

The posters were working: there had been two sightings of Spider so far, and he was quietly confident his dog was still in the area. A farmer had called the previous afternoon, and told him he'd seen a black and white mongrel, scavenging with a fox. Phil had taken Tom out there on his moped, and they'd scouted the lanes round about, and put up more notices. They would go out again that evening, to follow up the other report, which was from a woman in a nearby village. She'd phoned to complain: she'd seen a dog similar to the one in the photo worrying the ducks. Tom had to hope and pray Spider would stay where he was—the thought of him crossing roads by himself brought tears to the boy's eyes.

"You go to school," said Phil. "As soon as you're home, we'll get out there."

"I want to go now."

"You can't. And don't tell your dad: what we're doing is illegal. I'm not licensed for passengers, Tom."

"I know that. Thank you."

Phil paused.

"I spoke to your mum as well," he said. I told her what's happening, and she—"

"It's none of her business. I'm not talking to her, Phil, and you can't make me. If she's unhappy about it, that's fine—she deserves to be."

"You need to talk to her," said Phil.

"Why?"

"Because... look at you. You're like a bomb at the moment, and you're going to explode. If you don't talk to her, or to your dad—or to someone—"

"What is there to say? I'm sick of talking."

"And the fight?"

"What fight? It wasn't a fight, I told you. It was rugby."

"Oh, come on! That's not what the school said. Who's the counsellor? What's his name?"

"Warburton, and he's useless."

"You've spoken to him?"

"No."

"Then listen to me, Tom. If you're being bullied, you need to speak to him. You don't have to put up with it."

Tom snorted.

Phil stared into his eyes, until the boy looked away. He pulled his blazer on and walked to the front door, pausing at the mirror.

The bruising had faded to a sick-looking yellow, and most people had stopped commenting on it. Robert Tayler always grinned triumphantly, but it hadn't been hard to keep out of his way—most of the time.

All Tom wanted was his dog. He could endure any amount of loneliness and misery at school if there was still a chance of finding Spider. Spider was out there, somewhere, waiting for him—and Tom would find him.

He sat at the front of the classroom, trying to concentrate.

It was the last lesson before break. This one was PSHE, and they were discussing the importance of relationships. The whole class was restless, for the worksheet seemed particularly patronizing.

The first question was: *What makes a good friend?* There was a smiley face on the left, and a sad face on the right.

Tom gritted his teeth, and started to sketch Spider in the margin.

"Hey, Lipman," said the boy next to him.

It was a whisper, for they were supposed to be working in contemplative silence. He drew the ears and muzzle, and started on the neck.

His neighbour hissed again, and nudged him.

"Lipman! You're wanted."

Tom looked round, and there was his enemy. Robert Tayler gave Tom a bright, friendly wave, and held up a note.

The teacher didn't notice because she was drawing a huge pie chart on the whiteboard, with her back to the class. The word *loyal* stood out in blue.

Rob saw his opportunity, and skimmed the paper forward. It landed on the floor, but a nearby girl picked it up and sneaked it on to Tom's desk.

Tom unfolded it.

That dog you lost, the note said. *It's black and white, isn't it?*

He turned around again and nodded. Then he mouthed the word "Why?"

Rob started writing again.

The next note said, *I think I saw him this morning.*

Tom felt his heartbeat change. His hands immediately became clammy, but he tried to stay calm.

He wrote *WHERE?* Then he scribbled the obvious, urgent question: *Are you sure it was Spider?*

The note went back to Rob, and the teacher just missed it. She had the board pen in her hand and was scanning the class.

"What else do we want our friends to be?" she asked.

"Truthful," said someone.

"Sexy," said someone else.

"No, let's keep it serious," said the teacher. "Let's be sensible, shall we? What else? What makes a really *good* friend?"

"They have to be trustworthy," said a girl.

"Oh, definitely. Tom, what are you thinking?"

"He wouldn't know, miss," said someone.

The back row sniggered, and the teacher ignored it. She looked at Tom, remembering that his name had been flagged up by email that very morning. He was someone to watch and support, so she smiled at him encouragingly, and asked, "What's the most important thing for you, Tom, when it comes to friendship?"

"I don't care, miss."

There was more laughter, and the teacher held up her hand.

"I'm sure you do," she said. "What a thing to say, Tom. Tell us what you're really thinking."

Tom sighed, wishing he hadn't spoken, and wondering how he could get out of the spotlight. The teacher looked genuinely interested, so he decided to say what he felt.

"Look," he said. "If you make a real friend, I think you should hang on to them, the same as... the same as the people in your family. You shouldn't ever let them go, because..."

"Because what?"

"Once they're gone, they're gone. If they betray you, or treat you badly: that's it. It's over."

"Really?"

"Yes."

"What, no forgiveness? Isn't that a bit harsh?"

"It's common sense," said Tom. "Maybe some people like being hurt, but I can do without it. I think..."

"What? Quiet, please—let's hear what Tom thinks. This is interesting."

"You're better off on your own, in the end."

"Well!" said the teacher. "That's a thoughtful, honest answer. But what does Tom really mean by being 'better off on your own'? Let's get into our groups, and feed back in five."

There was an instant stir of activity.

Group work meant relative freedom: you could turn round in your seat and have a nice conversation, so as the teacher went back to the board the noise level rose dramatically.

Tom was looking for Rob again, and saw that he had his head down and was scribbling hard.

He glanced up at Tom, and smiled. He put his pen down,

then, and folded the paper. It was easy to lob it forward, and Tom opened it with trembling hands.

Sorry, old buddy, said the note. *It was Spider, and he's roadkill. We passed him in the bus: black and white dog, flat as a pancake. Try not to cry, black-eyes.*

Tom read the words carefully, twice, and found that he was standing up. The paper was in his hand, and he was on his feet, reading it for the third time. Either the class had gone quiet, or he'd gone deaf.

Robert Tayler was looking straight at him.

"Don't blame me," Rob said. "I thought you should know the truth."

"What's wrong?" asked the teacher.

"He's had a shock, miss," said someone.

"He needs his mum."

"He's wet himself."

"Hush," said the teacher. "Sit down, please, Tom. Let's try to stay focused on what you said. 'Being alone' is quite an emotive phrase."

Tom was struggling to breathe. He was hot, and his feet felt too heavy to move. He took a pace forward and steadied himself against a table. Then he was at the door, and the handle felt cold in his hand. He heard his name being repeated, but he kept walking. All he could think about was the horror of what Rob had just told him. The teacher was calling loudly, but there was no point turning round or going back: he wouldn't be able to speak.

He staggered out into the corridor and went quickly past the science labs. There was a boys' toilet, and he stepped into it. A mirror showed him the same face as usual, but that was impossible because his insides were melting, and everything had changed. Did he want to sit down? No. Did he want to wash, or run cold water over his head? No, because there was no point doing anything ever again.

The note was there in his hand, and the words were big and clear. He turned the page over, and there were more on the back: *Dead dog*, they said, and there was a picture of a truck going over a mangled animal. Its mouth was turned down to look sad, and the artist had even planted it in a lake of crimson blood.

Tom could not cry.

There were no tears available, because the heat inside him had burnt them away. He would never cry again, for he was hollow. Spider was on the roadside, dead, and it was just as he had feared. You saw it all the time: dogs raced across the road, and were hammered flat on the tarmac. The wheels turned them to furry mats, and he'd sometimes wondered what happened to the bodies—if they got scraped up by the people whose job it was to clean the roads, or if other animals dragged them off for food. A sob rose from deep inside, but he swallowed it and left the toilets.

He chose a different corridor, and a teacher he didn't know glanced at him and stopped.

"Excuse me, young man," he said. "Where should you be?"

"Nowhere."

"What?"

"Nowhere, sir. Anywhere."

"Who's your tutor? What do you mean?"

Tom ignored him and set off again.

"Hey!" said the teacher. "Stop a moment, please. Why aren't you in class? Where are you going?"

Tom couldn't speak any more, so he didn't try. He kept moving, for he had no voice, and no interest in anyone's questions. He was aware of the teacher hurrying after him, but there was nothing the man could do. Tom could walk for ever, out of the building and out of the school. He could keep going for however long it took, until he got to some part of the country where there were high cliffs, and then he could step off the edge of the highest, straight into the abyss.

He found himself at the library and went inside. The teacher was still behind him, but he moved on past the displays, for he knew where he was going now. He went to the office, at the back, because that was where Mrs Mourna worked. He opened the door, hoping she'd be there, but knowing in his heart that she wouldn't be. He knew now that people disappeared when you needed them most: her chair was bound to be empty.

In fact, she was sitting at her desk.

"Tom," she said quietly.

The other teacher stayed back.

Mrs Mourna was wrapping a book in clear plastic. Her face changed, and she rose to her feet at once. He became aware only of the silence in the room.

"What's the matter, love?"

His eyes were wet. He was crying after all, and he could feel his face imploding as he made noises he had never made before. He held up the note, but Mrs Mourna didn't read it. She simply put her arms around him, and Tom clutched her as the tears gave way to deep, shuddering sobs. Reality crashed down harder than ever, for it had dawned on him that Spider really wasn't coming home. That meant home was emptier than ever—as empty as his heart, which had been emptied by forces he didn't understand but could still feel, draining his blood and leaving him weak. His mother had left his father, which meant she'd left *him*. Spider had left, too, and now he was dead.

He'd reached the end, and it was the end of the end of everything.

8

Spider had come to a road sign.

The dog gazed up at it, and felt the tickling in his ear that was now so familiar. The flea drank, and there was a tiny sigh, followed by the soft belch. It crawled on to an eyebrow.

"Recognize anything?" it said.

The sign showed a fat roundabout, with roads leading off in five different directions. There were five words floating round them, and Spider waited as his companion spelt out the letters.

"Do you recognize anything?" asked the flea.

"No," said the dog, at last. "I've never heard those words before. Never."

"One of them has to be your town. The question is: which one and which road?"

"Why do they all look the same?" cried Spider. "How do people know where they're going?"

"Maybe they don't."

"Let's follow the busiest and just hope it's the right one. Are you comfortable up there?"

"I'm fine, Spider. Your fur's got a real silky softness to it."

"As soft as Jesse's?"

"Oh, softer."

"She was a special fox, wasn't she?"

"One of the best."

Spider nodded sadly.

They stood in silence for a moment, then the dog took a deep breath and set off, following the grass verge to a sturdy crash barrier. Slipping under it, the two friends kept close to the kerb and, within a few hundred metres, found themselves at an even busier junction. A great concrete bridge flew high above their heads, carrying vehicles in a roaring stream. Spider trotted on, his eyes smarting from the overpowering fumes. He threaded his way cautiously, for there was no pavement. On and on he went, and the road took them through a vast jumble of car parks and sheds.

"Civilization," said the flea. "I say keep going."

Spider nodded. "It's a big place," he said. "It could be my town, but I don't see a school. I don't recognize anything yet."

"Well, we're only at the edge."

They trotted on, and the going got a little easier. There was a muddy track which was much softer than the unforgiving tarmac, and before long they spotted houses.

"Where is everybody?" said Spider. "Why aren't there any people?"

"They're at work, I imagine."

"There was a big park with gates. If we found that, I'd know exactly where I was."

"Let's aim for those trees, then. Go left."

Spider turned down a side street, but the trees turned out to be a small cluster in somebody's garden. A car rolled by, but after that it was ominously quiet. The two friends pressed on in silence, down a hill lined with lamp posts, and this took them to a row of shops. When they came to a crossroads, Spider felt a very soft pinch.

"Stop," said the flea.

"Why?"

"We could be in luck. Look up—look at the sign."

Spider raised his eyes and saw a flat, metal triangle. It had been bolted to a pole, and it had a bright red border. Within the border were the shapes of two children, painted in solid black. They were running somewhere, holding hands, so the flea spelt out the word beneath their feet.

"School," it said. "It's got the right colours, too."

"Maybe every school is red and black," said Spider. "For all I know, every boy in the world wears the same uniform."

"I don't think so," said the flea. "I was in a school briefly—on the back of a hedgehog. He'd been taken inside for some project, and the kids I saw were wearing blue. I think we're close."

Spider trotted on, and within five minutes they both heard the unmistakable sound of laughter. Spider started to run—he couldn't help himself—and the noise got louder. He turned into a wide driveway, and suddenly they were beside a long set of railings.

A hundred children were swirling over the grass, squealing with excitement. They were chasing balls, cheering wildly. The joy was infectious, and Spider found he was barking, but the hope faded in an instant, for he could see at once that the colours were wrong. There were greens and whites, and various greys. Red and black were conspicuously absent, and it was also obvious that the boys were much younger than Tom. Some of them had seen him and were coming over, but Spider hadn't the heart to make contact, and slipped quickly out of sight. A track took him on to a patch of wasteland, and he sat down, wincing at the pain in his pads.

"Don't despair," said the flea quietly. "This is when we have to be strong."

"I think we've come the wrong way."

"You don't know that, Spider."

"I feel it."

"I say keep going. These might still be the outskirts of the town. Is Tom's school very big?"

"I've no idea."

"If it is, it might be right in the centre. Like the duck pond was in the middle of that village."

"Which way is the centre?"

"That's what we have to find out. And look, Spider! Off to the right there's a railway line, on the other side of the fence."

"So what?"

"So that's good news. A railway line means trains, which is what Jesse remembered. She talked about seeing uniforms where the railway lines ended. Let's just follow the tracks—it can't be much further."

They soon found a gate they could squeeze under, and Spider clambered down through more scrub to the rails. He stepped

156

wearily on to the sleepers and forced himself onwards, following their graceful curve. Before long, there were walls on either side, and then the lines were multiplying. They passed more sheds and workshops, and a train came by. It was easy to avoid, and when another one approached in the opposite direction they got the distinct impression that they were getting to the very heart of the town. A third followed, clattering past at speed and blasting its horn.

"Hey," cried the flea. "Look! You can see where they're going. I think we've made it, Spider. This is exactly what Jesse described."

"I can see a church tower," said the dog.

"Is that good?"

"I recognize it. It's the same one, I'm sure! I saw it from the roof. Moonlight showed it to me."

"What were you doing on a roof?"

"I don't know, but it was the roof of my house—I climbed up and saw that church. This must be the place, flea! There are people, too! Look at them."

"But is this a school?"

"I think it must be. Look out for red and black uniforms."

Spider trotted on, the pain in his paws forgotten. He came to a long concrete platform, and he padded up the ramp. A train had just pulled in, and its doors hissed open. Suddenly, the platform was a heaving mass of bodies, and the dog pushed in among them, hunting for anyone in the right clothes. He skipped between people, desperate to find Tom or the boy he'd seen boarding the bus. Everyone seemed so much older, though, and he yelped in frustration. An elderly woman struggled past with a trolley, helped by a man, and Spider stopped dead.

"What?" said the flea.

Both figures were wearing black trousers and white shirts. The trousers had a narrow red stripe.

"No blazer," said Spider. "No lion. But... it's red and black."

"They're not children," said the flea. "Does that matter?"

"I don't know, but this isn't what I was expecting. Something's wrong."

Spider noticed then that the woman was staring back at him, and she didn't look friendly. For the first time it occurred to him that he might be mistaken for a stray: he had no collar, after all. He backed away, but as he did so he noticed a doorway, out of which two young men emerged, wearing dark jackets. Spider ran to them, barking with excitement. They turned on him angrily, and one of them cursed. Spider dodged quickly to the side, but he came almost at once to a set of barriers which blocked his way. People were pushing through, and there was a clicking and clunking as they presented tickets. The barriers were guarded by figures in the exactly the same clothes, and that was when Spider realized Jesse's mistake. She had seen the red and black of the station staff, and assumed it had something to do with Tom's school.

"Oh, no," he said softly. "She misunderstood."

He sat down, and the flea pinched him.

"I think you're right," it said.

"Dear old Jesse. She was trying to help, but she got confused. Why should a fox know what a school is? Oh, flea, it could still be miles away. This is hopeless."

The two friends were silent.

They wandered back along the platform, and watched as the train that had emptied filled up again. It rolled out of the station, and soon another replaced it. The lights came on, for it was getting dark. The passengers thinned into a slow trickle, which dried up altogether.

The flea moved down on to Spider's nose.

"You need to rest, old pal. You're exhausted."

Spider nodded.

He lay down on the concrete, and realized how thirsty he was. He was hungry again, too, and his paws were so numb he could no longer feel them. He was covered in dirt, and his tongue was parched and gritty.

The flea pulled at a hair gently.

"You're depressed," it said. "And you're bound to be, Spider."

"I think it's all over," said the dog.

The flea chuckled. "No," it said. "We just need a few hours' sleep. In the morning, we try again."

"Try what?"

"To find this wretched school. It might be round the corner, Spider, waiting for us. You never know."

"We might be in the wrong town, though. We could be farther away than when we started. You should get out while you can— before it's too late."

The flea was quiet for a moment.

"Get out where?" it said, at last. "Where would I go, Spider? You're my home now."

"I can't be."

"But you are."

"No. Top yourself up, and let's say goodbye. I think you should be on your way."

The flea stood absolutely still.

"Spider, wait," it said. "I don't get what you're saying. What's wrong?"

The dog said nothing. He closed his eyes and whined—there was nothing else he could do.

"OK," said the flea, at last. "I do understand—of course I do. You've had enough of me. That's what you mean, yes? You think we should go our separate ways. I told you to say that, if it was ever what you felt. Honesty is the best policy, always... and now you've said it."

There was another silence, and Spider felt the flea walk up his nose and down again.

"That's it then," it said. "I do what I'm told. I've been unwanted all my life, dog, so you're not going to hurt my feelings. I just thought we were getting on pretty well."

"We were."

"What's changed? Have I been bossy? Have I overdone it?"

"No. You've helped me, and I appreciate it, but... come on. You've got your own life to lead."

"And I'm leading it, pal. With you. You're a good, loyal, friendly animal, and I want you to find Tom. Why split up now? We can split up when you're back in his arms, and he's throwing those sticks for you."

Spider shook his head.

"No," he said.

"Why not?"

"Because everything I do leads to disaster," he cried. "Everyone who meets me seems to end up unhappy—it's like I'm cursed. First it was my master, then it was Moonlight. I spent one day with Jesse and look what happened to her! There are *other* animals, flea, and you deserve better. Don't you have a family?"

The flea sighed. "Several, but I don't see them."

"Why not?"

"Oh, it's complicated."

"What you need is a nice, normal creature, because if you stay with me you're going to end up hurt. I had a friend called Thread, the first friend I ever made. It warned me I was a failure—and that's exactly what I am."

"That was your friend, huh? A *friend* told you that?"

"Yes."

"A spider?"

"Yes."

The flea laughed.

"My God," it said quietly. "You've been listening to spiders? I don't believe it."

"This one told me the truth."

"I doubt that. It sounds terrible, Spider! It must have wrecked your confidence, because that's what spiders do. They're complete, total liars—everyone knows that. They make webs! They're stealthy. That's how they survive."

"Thread was different."

"Oh, for goodness' sake," cried the flea. "You are such an innocent. The world is complicated, my friend—and there are some species on this planet who deceive us, and enjoy doing so. Spiders are the worst! Where does it live?"

"In Tom's bedroom," said Spider. "Up in the skylight."

"And it would eavesdrop, I imagine?"

"What does that mean?"

"It means it'd listen in on conversations, like a spy. Then it'd float down and pretend to know everything, and interfere—yes?"

"He was very friendly," insisted Spider. "He invited me to his home once."

"Did you go?"

Spider nodded.

"What was it like?"

"Not very nice," said the dog. "He'd caught a little moth, and he was playing with him. Torturing him, really."

"Exactly! You see? That's what they do! I've met so many spiders in my time, and there might be exceptions, but they're generally sadistic, solitary and desperately unhappy. They lie for the pleasure of lying, and they feed off the misery of others. I tell you something: when we get to Tom's place, I'll sort him out. He won't try that nonsense with me. Now I'm a parasite—"

"No, that's not true—"

"Of course it's true! Look at me. I don't like the word, but I will never pretend to be what I'm not. And I don't claim to be useful, but at least I'm not deadly, or poisonous—and I *don't* get pleasure out of grief."

The flea took a deep breath and sighed.

"I choose life," it said. "And perhaps I'm going to speak out of turn. You can shut me up or shake me off, and if you want me to go, I'll go—I'm a flea, after all, and you're not going to miss me—but there's something we have in common."

"What?"

"We believe in what's good. We believe in sticking together. You're not going to rest until you find Tom, and that's what I love about you, Spider: you have a purpose, and that's why your blood is so rich. I've never been happier."

Spider said nothing. He was aware of his friend moving to the tip of his nose. The next moment, it had vaulted straight upwards and was on the ground between his paws. It gazed up at him with fierce, serious eyes.

"Do I stay or go?" it asked.

"Flea," said Spider, "I don't want to cause you pain."

"Well, that's going to be hard, because the world's full of it—as we both know."

Spider was silent again.

"Come on, dog!" cried the flea. "Let's cut to the chase here, because we need a plan. Are we together, on a mission? Or are we finished?"

Spider twitched his ears back and blinked. He put his muzzle so close to the flea that the little insect suddenly seemed huge. Its big eyes were moist, and its antennae were trembling with emotion.

"Stay," said the dog softly.

"Are you sure?"

"I'm sure. And… thank you. Thank you for helping me."

The dog gazed down the empty platform, too tired to move, and thought of Tom. He thought of the park and the lead and Tom's soft, comfortable bed.

Closing his eyes, he didn't notice the shadow as it fell across him. He didn't even pick up the scent, for he was just too tired— and the flea's tiny scream came seconds too late.

A boot clamped down hard on Spider's tail, pinning him to the ground. Even as he tried to scramble up, a gloved hand pressed a weapon to his shoulder, and a jolt of electricity sent him into yelping convulsions. The second blast hit him full in the chest, and knocked him unconscious.

9

Spider came round to find that his paws were tied together.

When he went to moan, he felt something round his mouth, and realized it was the same kind of restraint that bound his legs: it was a plastic strip, pulled tight, and there was another connected to it, under his ears. There was no way of chewing them, for his jaws were sealed. Worst of all, there was a throbbing pain in every muscle. He was on a sheet of old, stinking cardboard.

"Are you awake?" asked the flea.

Spider had never known such relief. He wasn't alone: his friend was still there, deep in his ear.

"You've been out a long time, Spider. It's morning, and we're in trouble. Can you speak at all? Take it easy."

Spider managed a thin whisper. "Where are we?"

"It's a garage of some kind. He unloaded us late last night and locked us in."

"Why? Who is he?"

"I don't know."

"I can smell other dogs. Cats, too—are we on our own?"

"Yes."

"It's the laboratory, I bet. Did he say anything?"

"No, but I'm still hopeful, Spider. I think he might work for a rescue centre, or something like that. We were put in a van, so it must be his job to gather in stray animals. When the owners come looking, you get reunited: that's what I'm hoping."

"So why am I tied up? I'm so thirsty, flea. This is terrible! We have to get out."

"I know it's hard, Spider, but there's nothing we can do at the moment. We have to sit it out and cooperate. We have to stay optimistic."

"He's coming back."

"Now? How can you tell?"

Spider whined in fear. "I can hear his boots," he said. "I don't like him, and I don't trust him—"

"OK, but stay calm! Don't try to fight or he'll just zap you again."

"Oh, Tom... Where are you?"

The flea tugged at a hair, and pinched him.

"Keep calm," it hissed. "Tom is looking for you, even now. Don't forget that."

Heavy footsteps were definitely approaching, and there was a jangle of keys. A door opened with a metallic screech, and the early-morning sun hit Spider right between the eyes. He squirmed in terror, for there were now two men standing over him, and they were shoulder to shoulder. The grip around his paws was merciless, and all he could do was shudder.

"He's fine," said the first, after a short silence.

"Good," said the second. "I thought he might be too skinny. You definitely want him?"

"Why not? The more the merrier."

Spider writhed again, but he couldn't quite see their faces. They were dark shapes, and they smelt of sweat.

"Any ID? Have you checked?"

"Nothing at all. No collar, no chip. He's only a few months old, so he's been abandoned, I imagine. Unwanted gift."

"That's what we like."

"Long legs."

"Young and tender."

Spider felt a boot under his ribs. He was turned over, and one of the men squatted close. A hand pulled at his fur, and he managed a yelp of panic.

"It's the coat I noticed," said the man. "I thought it had a certain softness. Loose skin as well—feel it."

"Forget it. I'm not dealing in fur."

"Since when?"

"Since I got caught, mate. There's no money in it, anyway—not at this end."

Spider gazed up, totally confused. Both figures were sturdy, and the stink of cigarettes was overpowering. There was a sudden scent of leather, too, for one was pulling out a wallet, and Spider glimpsed banknotes. The first man's mouth twisted into a thin smile as he pocketed them, while the other hauled on a pair of large gauntlets. The stench of dirty rubber made Spider gasp—there was old blood in the mix, too. Seconds later, the gloves were under his forelegs, and though he tried to twist, he didn't stand a chance. He was lifted up, as the other man hauled a wire cage from the side and opened it under him. He bucked, but there was no point: the hands were strong, and one grabbed his tail to force him through the gap head first. He collapsed on to a hard steel tray, and the two men lifted him together. Spider started to shake. He hadn't noticed the truck, for it had been parked some distance away, but now he could hear the engine. Its shutter was up and open, and as he approached the darkness within, Spider heard volleys of barks and a terrified whimpering.

"Stay calm," hissed the flea.

"How?"

"You just have to."

"Where are we going? Where are they taking us?"

"Be brave, Spider. I'm not leaving you. If it's a dogs' home, we'll be fine, so—"

"But we're prisoners!"

"Shhhh!"

The flea was shaking, too. It moved swiftly to Spider's neck and clung there as they were loaded into the truck.

In the gloom they could see rows of cages, jammed haphazardly on top of each other. They could make out anxious eyes, too, and there was a chorus of agonized howling. Paws rattled at bars, but the men took no notice at all. One of them leapt into the vehicle and started to organize things. The howling grew louder, and Spider's cage was forced into a gap between a slender spaniel, which was lying on its side, and what might have been a bulldog. A chain rattled over their heads, and a padlock clicked shut. The man's face came close, and Spider saw that despite the gloom he

167

was wearing sunglasses. He saw his own terrified reflection in the lenses. The cage door opened, and a knife touched his throat.

Spider had no time even to yelp, and he felt fingers close to his windpipe.

The flea clutched his fur.

"Stay still," it hissed. "It's only for the plastic. He's taking the plastic off!"

The first band was cut neatly in half. It fell from Spider's mouth, and he sighed with relief. The man's hands moved to his paws, and suddenly his legs were free. He struggled to his feet, poised to spring through the door—as it snapped shut in his face.

"I can smell death," whimpered Spider. "It's all around us!"

"I know."

He had just enough room to stay upright, but could only turn with difficulty. The man had vaulted out of the truck and was disappearing round the side. The shutter started to close, clanking as it came down. The light was fading.

"OK," said someone. "Hold tight, guys—it looks like we're moving."

Spider wormed himself around again, and saw the outline of the dog he'd glimpsed earlier. It was actually a pit bull, with broad, powerful shoulders, and its face was pressed to the wire, peering in at him.

"Are you hurt?" it barked. "What's your name, pal?"

"Who?" yelped someone.

"We've got a newcomer here. Last one in, I reckon."

There was a frantic scratching from further down the line, and a hoarse panting from underneath.

"We need to know where we're going," said a voice. "Does anyone know for sure?"

"Please," said someone else, "I need food. I really do need food…"

"Has anyone got water?"

"Down here, guys. We've lost another one…"

Spider said nothing at all. He inched his body round in another tight circle, and saw that the dog on his other side hadn't moved—and wasn't going to. A few cages below, a creature was gnawing at the wire, but the worst sound of all was the continuous howling: it was the screech of cats as well as dogs, rising in volume as the truck's engine revved madly, and the vehicle started to shake.

"I'll go and explore," said the flea.

"Don't!" said Spider. "Don't leave me."

"We have to get some answers," whispered the flea. "Keep calm, OK? I'll be back."

"You won't find me!"

"I will, Spider—trust me. I won't desert you, so stay still. Save your energy."

Spider whined, and saw his friend leap out into the gloom. His neck was twisted, pressing against the mesh, and he could smell the pit bull's bitter breath as it panted. That's when he realized his cage had shifted, and they were now nose to nose.

"Take it easy, pal," it said quietly. "You're safe."

"Am I?" asked Spider.

"You're going to be fine, buddy. We're being looked after."

Spider tried to retreat, but there was nowhere to go. He gazed at his neighbour and shuddered. In all his short, protected life, he had never seen a creature so mauled and disfigured. He went to speak, but no words came.

"What?" said the pit bull. It flexed the muscles across its chest and put its huge head on one side. "What are you looking at, boy?"

"Nothing," whispered Spider.

"No?"

"No. Just trying to get my bearings."

"That won't be easy," growled the pit bull. "You're the last man in, I think. We made a detour for you, pal—you only just made it."

Spider blinked and tried to breathe normally. The animal's voice was deep and coarse, and its teeth were broken stumps. The nose was blunt and crushed, and Spider saw that the right eye was completely missing. There was no fur anywhere, either: just pale, bruised skin stretched over a dented skull. He knew the dog was female, and he remembered meeting a similar breed in the park. This one clearly needed help—an ear had been bitten to a stump—but she stood in her cage, as firm as a rock.

"Buster's the name," she said. "What happened to you? You look bad."

"I got caught," said Spider.

"Who by?"

"By one of those men. He had a gun, I think."

"That's not a gun, buddy—that's a cattle prod. Were you lost or left?"

"I don't know. Lost, I think."

"That's too bad. A lost dog is a sad dog, and that's what I am, too—lost as lost can be. Pleased to meet you, by the way."

"Pleased to meet you…"

"What's your name?"

"Spider."

"Buster."

"I was trying to get home, Buster—back to my master."

"Is he looking for you?"

"Yes."

"You don't have to worry, then. I've got a whole load of people, thank goodness—they'll be out looking for me right now, so it's just a question of time. That's why I'm not making a fuss, you see? No point fighting this. What's your name?"

"Spider. I just told you. I—"

"I'm Buster. It's a boy's name, of course, but I'm used to it now. When d'you get caught?"

"Yesterday, I think, but I'm a bit confused."

"Me too. Ha!"

As the pit bull spoke, there was a crunch of gears. Everyone shifted forward, and a cage further down was tipped on to the one below. There was a desperate yapping, and a renewed howl of fear.

"Hold tight, eh?" said Buster.

Spider wedged himself into a corner, and his neighbour chuckled.

"I don't know how they work, the old cattle prods," she said. "They stun the brain, I imagine, and they got me right in the neck. It's what they use, these guys, and you don't have a chance—there's no biting back. I've been here a while... Watch out now!"

They were swinging slowly round a corner. Spider felt his own cage sliding backwards.

"I was trying to keep a record of the days," continued Buster. "You know what I mean? Scratches on the floor, because... Listen." She lowered her voice, and the growl was deep and soft. "That's the main thing, friend: in a situation like this you need to keep up the old self-discipline. You mustn't go to pieces, or get yourself isolated. I like to keep in shape, but this driver can't exercise us—or he doesn't want to, maybe."

"Who is he?"

"No idea. But he's in charge at the moment."

"There's a really bad smell in here, Buster."

"I know. Take shallow breaths—that's what I do, because there's been casualties and there might be more."

"Where's he taking us? Does anyone know?"

"Not for sure, but I'm hoping it's a home."

"A dogs' home?"

"A pet centre—to, you know, keep us safe. My owner might be there already, if I'm lucky."

They were accelerating. The road had straightened, and there was a breeze running through the truck.

"We have to find out for sure," said Spider quietly. "I think it could be one of those laboratories, and if it is we have to do something."

"I don't believe in labs. I heard the tales, but they never made sense."

"They do experiments in them."

"Who do?"

"I don't know, Buster! I don't *want* to know!"

"Ah, they're just scare stories, pal—to frighten the pups. If you want to know what I think: I think we're off to a good old refuge or something similar. That's what some of the cats were saying, and it's logical. We've been cleared off the streets, OK? They have to do that, these guys, so I figure they must have a place in mind. And here's another thing: we got sprayed down last night with a hosepipe. We all got a drink, so maybe he's not so bad, this driver. No food yet, but it'll come. Where did they find you?"

"I was at the railway station."

"Really? Which one?"

"I don't know!"

"I've been to most of them, over the years. I used to be up and down on the old railways—quite a regular. Sorry, I asked your name, but I've forgotten it. My memory's just about gone, you see. You can guess what I do, huh?"

"No." Spider shook his head. "No idea, Buster. What do you do?"

"Ah, come on! Look at me."

The dog put her head on one side and showed her teeth. Her breath was worse than ever, and the empty eye socket was pink and raw.

"What does a dog like me do for a living?" she asked.

"I honestly don't know," said Spider nervously. "Were you a guard dog, maybe?"

"Ah, you're warm."

"You're not one of those police dogs that looks for explosives, are you? Like a—"

"Sniffer dog? No way. Guess again—last guess."

"I don't know, really I don't—"

"I'm an attack dog, pal: I fight for money. I did some breeding when I was a youngster, but that's over now. It's been one scrap after another lately—and that's what worries me, you see, because I'm key. I'm part of a team, and I have a boss and a schedule and… they'll be going crazy right now. It's against every rule in the book."

"What is?"

"Getting lost! You don't get lost—ever. You stay close to your master, so you're there when you're needed, and… Sorry."

"What?"

The pit bull was twitching. She closed her one good eye and retched.

"What's wrong?" asked Spider.

"Nothing. I just... I get the shakes sometimes. Flashbacks, too... Where was I? What's your name?"

"It's Spider, Buster. You were talking about staying close to your master."

"That's the only rule, really. Don't get separated, because when the man in charge needs you, that's when he needs you."

Spider nodded, feeling worse than ever. The truck picked up speed, and the pit bull shook herself violently and barked a laugh.

"I'd been taking a few hits lately," she said. "Quite a few, if I'm honest. You know, losing bets? I don't have the speed I used to have. I was looking forward to the next fight, though, and we were going up north—I was in the zone, ready for anything. And I still don't know what happened, but we didn't ever get there. All of a sudden, Spider—listen to this—the door of the van came open, right? And I felt a great big foot under the you-know-what. A boot, Spider—like I was sitting on the boss's foot. You ever do that?"

"What?"

"What I just said: sit on your master's foot."

"Well, yes, I think so—"

"It's puppy stuff, yeah? We've all done it—of course we have—but I thought I'd grown out of it. Anyway, the next thing I knew, up it came and I was lifted up and out—I was kicked down the blasted road. Wham-bam! I was rolling down the motorway and ended up in the gutter all covered in blood. How did that happen?"

Buster barked again, and Spider cowered back in his cage.

"Didn't he stop?" he asked.

"Who?"

"Your owner, Buster. Didn't they pull over and wait for you?"

"I don't think anyone saw," said the pit bull quietly. "They just

174

drove off faster—top speed, in fact. All I heard was laughter. And here I am, with the lost and the lonely! Watch out, pal... we're slowing down."

Sure enough, the truck was braking again. The cages shifted, and Spider braced himself with his legs and his head, fearing that the whole pile would topple at any moment. Again, there were cries of panic.

"What do *you* do?" hissed Buster.

She was further away now, but Spider could still see her mad, blinking eye. He could hear her claws, too, as she stomped her paws on the metal.

"I don't do anything," he said.

"No? What are you, then?"

"I'm an ordinary dog. I'm very lost and very scared."

"Ah, you're a pet! I've forgotten your name again, pal—I had it, but it's gone."

"Spider."

"I'm forgetting more and more, Spider—getting old, I guess, and... I've started drooling a bit, but that's under control. You know, some say we're on different sides, the pros and the pets. I don't believe that: I keep the fighting for the ring."

Spider nodded weakly.

"First fight I ever had," she said, "they put me up against some mongrel-monster twice my size, and he cut me up pretty bad. He was stronger, and he got the taste of blood, so what I did was: I whimpered around a bit, played up like a girl, and he thought he had me. He was on top, and that's when I turned and went for the windpipe. Never looked back after that. Who's looking for you? You say someone's out there, searching?"

"I hope so, Buster. He's called Tom."

"Is that your master? Tom?"

Spider nodded sadly. Just saying the name made his heart ache, and he had to stifle a whine.

"You stay with Tom, buddy," said the pit bull. "Don't let him go."

Spider howled quietly. "I didn't mean to let him go, Buster! And I was so close to finding him—or I might have been."

"He'll be waiting for you, won't he? Mine will."

"Will he, though? There was a misunderstanding, and I ran away. He may have replaced me by now, and—"

"Hey, now. Don't say that!"

"He might, though! I was a bad dog. I let him down."

"No," said Buster. "No. You mustn't think negative thoughts, OK? You must hold on to what you have. No dog is replaceable, ever: that's what I believe. That's why I feel for the boss—he's going to be in pieces right now, worrying about me. He'll be driving round, putting up posters…"

The pit bull shook her head and barked.

"Has Tom put up posters? That's what they do, you see, if they really want you back. Posters saying 'Missing dog' and a nice picture, with their phone number slap-bang under it. Has your guy done that?"

Spider went to speak, but found he couldn't. He stood in his cage, frozen to the spot, and the pit bull stared at him.

"What's the matter?" she asked.

"Oh, God," groaned Spider.

"You're shivering, pal. Are you getting cold?"

"That's exactly what he's done! I thought he might want me punished, but the posters are just asking people if they've seen me. He *is* looking for me, Buster. He's *missing* me!"

"Then you have to hold on, don't you? We're both OK, Spider!

We're going to be found soon, and it's going to be some reunion!"

Even as the pit bull spoke, the driver was braking harder than ever. Spider's cage was tilting badly, but he didn't care. Suddenly, he felt light-headed with hope. He jumped at the cage door, butting it with his nose. The stack bulged in the centre, and as the truck took a bend the whole pile tumbled, and everything slid forward. Spider's cage rolled over, and he lay on his back, too stunned to move.

When his eyes focused, he saw that he had new neighbours. There was an elderly lurcher, whimpering to itself with its eyes tight shut. Closer, though, was a smaller cage that had landed on its side, and cowering in the furthest corner was a slim, silver cat. She was mewing and turning in tight circles, so for a moment Spider didn't recognize her. Then she stood still, and he glimpsed the stump of a tail. He saw her profile, too, and realized with a shock that the face he remembered so well was horribly thin. The bony shoulders suggested starvation.

"Moonlight?" he hissed.

He kept his voice low, but he saw her eyes widen in fear.

"Moonlight, it's me," he said. "You remember me, don't you?"

"Spider?" said the cat. "Surely not—it can't be." Her voice was a croak.

"It *is* me, Moonlight! What are you doing here?"

"It can't be you, darling…"

"What's happened to you?"

The cat inched forward and put her nose against the wire.

"Oh, Spider," she said. "Oh, my dear, true love. The bravest dog I ever knew. Oh, my angel. I… I thought I heard your voice earlier, but I assumed it was just another dream tormenting me. You've come to rescue me, haven't you? You've followed me! I knew you would, Spider. But where are they taking us?"

As she spoke, the truck shunted forward, and they heard the clang and scrape of heavy gates on concrete. The cages shook, and a shower of fleas dropped through the bars and hopped madly over the floor. Spider felt one on his eyebrow, and knew that his own had returned—he felt it shift to the safety of his ear.

He twisted round, for the cat was now behind him. Buster's cage was on its side, some distance away, and he could hear the pit bull gnawing at the wire.

They were plunged into darkness.

"Moonlight!" he cried. "I'll try to get help—don't worry."

"We've got problems," hissed the flea.

"I know, but I've just found an old friend, and listen, flea—I've had good news."

"No, Spider, *you* listen—"

"Tom's out there, looking for me! The poster we saw said 'Missing Dog' and it had his phone number! He wants me back!"

"Spider, stop talking!"

"Why?"

"Because we're in terrible danger, and I was wrong. Tom's not going to find you—not where we're going. We need to do something—fast."

Spider could hear something in the flea's voice he'd never heard before. He could feel its tiny body trembling as it searched for the words. The truck was rolling forward down a steep slope and a bell was ringing.

"Spider," hissed the flea, "there are fleas in this truck that have made this trip before, and you need to know the truth. This is a *McKinley's* lorry, from the factory—"

"What factory? What do you mean?"

178

"McKinley's Foods," said the flea. "You've heard of them, haven't you? Every animal has heard of McKinley's—they make those awful pet snacks."

"I've heard the name, yes. I've seen a box, I think."

There was a screech of brakes as he spoke, and the fresh air was replaced by a thick stink of boiling fat. Spider found he was retching, and the animals around him started to splutter and howl. He was plunged back in time to a hungry evening when he'd been foraging for food. It was the same evening he'd climbed a tree in search of a squirrel, and he remembered the brightly coloured carton, with smears of something foul. He'd forced himself to sniff at it—and that was the smell in his nostrils now.

"It's a meat factory," said the flea.

"Meat?" cried Buster from the back of the truck. "So they're feeding us! What did I tell you, guys? We're going to be OK!"

"No. You don't understand," said the flea. Spider could feel the insect trembling still as it struggled to speak. "Oh, Spider! McKinley's makes pet food out of unwanted pets. *You're* the meat, Spider! You're all going to be slaughtered, and we've left it too late…"

As the flea's words died away, the steel shutter started to rise. Floodlights blazed, and the animals were blinded.

PART THREE

1

"It wasn't my fault," said Phil. "You know it wasn't, Tom—and I'm not going to let you blame me for a whole load of accidents and misunderstandings. I've tried to help you find him, and what you're saying isn't fair."

"He should have been outside, in the garden."

"Yes. I made a mistake."

"You certainly did. None of this would have happened if you'd put him out, which is what you're supposed to do before you go to your stupid college."

Phil said nothing.

"You're supposed to help us," said Tom quietly. "That's the only reason Dad lets you stay here. You pay a cheap rent, and the whole place stinks of your bloody bits of bike—and you didn't check. You let Spider have the run of the house, and that's why he went crazy. He chewed up my room, which meant Dad threw him out. It's all because of you, Phil. You killed my dog."

Tom sat at the kitchen table, and Phil stood at the sink looking at him.

"But you don't know he's dead," said Phil.

"He's been run over."

"Tom—"

"Robert Tayler *saw* him. Saw him in the road. I'm not going to forgive you. I think you should move out."

Phil went to speak, and thought better of it. There was another silence.

"Who is Robert Tayler?" he asked, at last. "Is he a friend?"

"I don't have friends."

"Yes, you do."

"Not any more. When do I see them? When do I have *time* to see them? Tayler's my worst enemy: he hates me, and I hate him."

"Right. So what if he's just making it up? What if he wrote the note to upset you? It's what people do sometimes."

"I don't."

"Don't you? You never try to hurt people by lashing out?"

Phil pulled out a chair. As he sat down, the phone started to ring and they both stared at it.

"I'm not answering it," said Tom.

"I didn't expect you to."

"Why don't *you*?"

"She doesn't want to speak to me. She wants you. She wants to hear your voice—that's why she calls."

"Well, she's not going to have that pleasure, is she?"

"One word, buddy. Pick up the phone, and—"

"I'm not talking to her ever again. I don't need her, and I don't need you. She walked out on us, Phil! She decided to leave us, and you can't make me speak to her, because you're not even family. You're just some guy who moved in because Dad lost his job, and..."

"What? Go on. Say it."

"And you're a parasite. You talk to her if you're so into reconciliations. Tell her we're all fine and happy, having a wonderful time."

Phil shook his head, and the answerphone clicked in. They both listened, waiting for the voice. They heard breathing, and that intake of breath when someone tries to speak and fails to find the words. They listened as she failed again.

The door opened, and Tom closed his eyes.

"What's the time?" asked his father.

Phil checked his watch, and the machine turned itself off.

"Eight twenty-five, nearly."

"That was your mum?"

"Yes," said Tom.

He crossed over to the kettle and switched it on. They all waited as it reboiled, noisily. Phil handed him a mug, and Dad made himself tea.

"Where's your tie?" he said, at last.

"It's in my pocket," said Tom.

"You shouldn't be here, should you? You need to put your tie on and get going. Is that a clean shirt? It looks—"

"I don't have a clean shirt, Dad—I never do. The washing machine's broken."

"Again?"

"Again."

"Oh."

"That's just what I said," said Tom. "When it broke."

There was another silence. Tom's father sat down.

"We can still do the laundry, you know. It just means… organisation. Let's get going, and we'll sort it tonight."

"I'm not going anywhere. I'm staying here."

Tom's dad added some sugar and sipped again. Tom stared at a spoon, and another silence stretched between them, unbreakable. Outside, a builder chose the moment to hammer at a piece of wood, and they found themselves listening as he drove home the nails: every blow ricocheted twice, and then it was so quiet again that it hurt.

Phil's phone bleeped, but he ignored it.

"Your school is the best there is," said Tom's dad. "We chose it together. You worked for that exam, and you passed it easily, and you're doing well. You're clever, and you enjoy it… or you used to."

Tom said nothing, so his father sipped his drink and swallowed.

"It's an adjustment—of course it is."

"I don't have any friends."

"Tom, we talked about this. You told us you wanted a new start and a whole new challenge—that's what you said, and we didn't push you."

"Mum did."

"Did she? She encouraged you, yes. Because she—"

"Because she what?"

"Believed in you. As she still does, just as I still do. Phil does—everyone does. And what happened with the dog was a terrible thing, but we have to get past it and move on."

Tom went to speak, but found that this time he couldn't.

"You're not a baby any more," said his father. "Things change, and there are some things in this world that we have to face. We have to cope with what life throws at us. If you don't go to school, you'll fall behind and become more miserable. What do you want to do? Sit there all day and feel angry? I'll buy you another dog."

Tom put his hands over his face.

"I will, Tom, if—"

"I don't want another dog, and I don't want anyone. Why were you so cruel? Is that why people leave all the time? Because of you?"

Dad put down his cup.

"Maybe," he said. "Why do you ask?"

"Because I want to leave, too. I want to get out of here and never come back. I can't stand it here."

"I'm sorry. But people leave because things go wrong. Sometimes we break, Tom. I break because I'm not a saint—I'm human, like you. And right this minute I'm on the very edge—so is she—"

"Where did she go? Where is she?"

"I can't answer that."

"You don't know?"

"Mum needed some space, whatever that means. And if you need to ask questions, you should just talk to her, because all you're doing at the moment is hurting yourself. It can't go on."

Nobody spoke. The builder started drilling.

"I'm not having you sitting there all day. Listen to me, Tom. I'm going to go upstairs. By the time I get back, you will have walked out of here and you will be on your way to school. Blow your nose, please. Get your bag. And get yourself moving."

Tom sat back in his chair as his dad left the room.

He watched as Phil walked to the kitchen door in silence, bolting it shut. That meant he would be leaving soon. He would go up to his room first, to get a few bits and pieces, and then he would ride away. His keys were on the counter, because he picked them up last, and Tom stared at the long, silver one, aware that his stomach had contracted. Sweat prickled under his arms, and he started to breathe faster. He waited for Phil to reach the landing. He could hear his father in the bathroom, so there was no time to lose.

The moped was right outside the house, and Tom had the keys in his hand. If he wore the crash helmet, nobody would see that he was too young to be riding. He knew how to control the thing because Phil had let him play on it in the garden, and he even had five pounds in his pocket should he need fuel. He opened the front door, pulling his coat over his blazer—the zip went right up to the chin, so the red and black were concealed. There was nothing to stop him now, except the fear of getting caught—and why should he care about that? School was over—he would never go back. If he ended up in jail, what did it matter?

He would scour the roads and find out the truth, for something had clicked into place. It was something Phil had said—about Robert Tayler, and the need to cause upset, or pain. It had brought back the memory of the boy's evil smile. He'd been grinning even as he wrote his note, and he'd gazed at Tom as he opened it. Phil hadn't been there, but he'd known instinctively, and he—Tom— had been stupidly slow. He had swallowed a lie, and if that was the case, Spider was alive and well, and needed to be found.

He closed the door and eased the bike off its stand. It was heavier than he remembered, and more awkward, but he got it down and steadied it. The helmet was bright yellow, locked to a bar by the saddle: he freed it and slipped it over his head. All he had to do now was mount the thing and fire the motor, but his hands were trembling so violently that he couldn't turn the key. Finally, he managed it: the motor roared, and he only just remembered how to engage the brake.

Surely Phil would hear the noise? He would recognize the sound of his own bike and burst out of the house. Tom pulled the throttle back, hard, and lifted his feet. The next second he'd swerved into the middle of the road, hauling the handlebars round just in time. He wobbled and veered sideways, braking again. Then he accelerated harder than ever, and was gone.

Nobody gave chase.

Phil heard the door close, and so did Tom's father.

They came down to the kitchen together, relieved to find it empty. They assumed the boy was being sensible, and didn't realize that the moped keys were missing for another twenty minutes. They had another cup of tea together, agreeing that Tom would get over his loss soon and things would get better. By the time Phil discovered the theft, Tom was on the ring road.

2

The truck's shutter had lifted completely, and the workers stood ready. Spider gazed in horror, trying to take in his new surroundings.

The rear of the truck fitted snugly into the bay, and amber lamps gave the world a sickly glow. A bell was still ringing, and he could hear the violent drumming of wheels as a conveyor belt cranked into life. Those waiting wore identical white overalls and their eyes peered out over face masks, so you couldn't tell if they were men or women. What scared Spider most, though, were their bright red gauntlets—he could smell a powerful disinfectant, but under it was the unmistakable scent of blood.

As he looked on, whimpering, two of the figures leapt into

the truck and set about their work. They disentangled the cages, using their boots to kick them into line. Then they lifted them, one at a time, and hurled them out of the vehicle. They didn't need to sort them. Nobody looked inside, for nobody cared about individual animals. The cages were flung from one worker to the next, and there were cheers as they bundled them towards the conveyor belt.

Spider had no idea where Moonlight was, for his own cage had been thrown to one side and he'd lost all sense of direction. The next moment, he felt hands lifting him up and he was pitched through the air. When he was slammed down again the breath was knocked from his body.

The flea was gripping the dog's fur for dear life.

"Spider!" it cried. "Do something!"

"Go," gasped the dog.

"Go where?"

"Save yourself! Jump!"

Dazed and desperate, Spider got his head up and glimpsed what lay ahead. He was on the conveyor. It was moving slowly into the factory's dark mouth, and he could feel the heat of an oven. In the distance there was a small, square hatch that every cage would pass through. The bell had stopped ringing, and there was now a low, mechanical grinding, while the belt still groaned and squeaked. Suddenly a buzzer sounded. The motors changed up a gear, and there was a scream that left Spider cowering. The unloading was complete—he could see that—and the belt was accelerating. Moonlight appeared for a moment, two cages ahead of him, and he realized that he hadn't even said goodbye. He searched for Buster, twisting painfully in his prison, but seconds later he was through the hatch, and was plunged into inky blackness. The flea was still in his ear, pinching hard even as it shook.

Spider felt a change in direction, and he pawed at the wire. He barked and attacked the cage with his teeth. He lashed out with his claws, but they were blunt and useless. On he went, into the light again, and now he could hear pulleys above. The lamps were mercilessly bright, and the world had expanded into a great white chamber covered in gleaming tiles. Spider looked left and right, trying to work out what was happening. He could see cables overhead, stretched between slowly turning wheels. There were hooks, too, dangling at intervals—he saw one dip low on its chain and pluck the first cage up neatly by its handle.

All at once, he understood—and he realized there was nothing the animals could do.

The first cage was lifted into the air and carried onwards and upwards, higher and higher. Then the second cage was lifted, and then the third. He heard a click as his own cage was plucked up off the belt, and he found himself swinging as the pulleys squeaked cheerfully. It was getting hotter, and Spider saw the future in all its terrifying detail. The pulleys were hauling the cages ever closer to the source of the heat, which was an enormous vat—its iron cover had been folded back, and steam billowed upwards. The first cage disappeared into the murk, and the final stage of the sequence was all too obvious. The cages would pass over the container and they would be flipped upside down, the doors opening automatically as the cables tightened. Every pet would be shaken loose and dropped into whatever was boiling beneath them.

Spider found that he was scrabbling at the wire again, just like every other creature in the line.

Moonlight was yowling, but the most insistent voice was the one deep inside the dog's ear.

"Use your tooth, Spider!" cried the flea. "Use the long one!"

"How?"

"I don't know, but it's our only chance!"

Spider attacked the mesh harder than ever, but the cage was simply rocking, and he was still a prisoner. The stench engulfed him, and for a moment he thought he'd pass out. He was aware of other fleas jumping for their lives—and that was the moment he glanced behind and saw hope.

Buster had freed herself.

She was five cages behind, and by some miracle she had bitten through part of the mesh. The old dog's mouth was cut, and her one good eye was flashing with fury. Somehow she had gnawed her way through solid steel, tearing open a hole through which she now hauled her scarred, twisted body. As Spider watched, she dragged herself on to the roof of her cage and got ready to leap. With astonishing grace, her back legs launched her through the air, and she grabbed the cage in front. She clung to it as it swung wildly, and a quick push with her blunt, bloody nose sprang the catch so that the gate fell sideways. A young puppy jumped for its life.

Inspired, Spider tried again, straining with his muzzle and working his long tooth at the loop that sealed him in. Buster appeared above him just as he succeeded. The door popped open, and he was out, steadied for a moment by the pit bull's powerful shoulder.

He was free.

Now he could try the same manoeuvre as his friend. His paws scrabbled, but he jumped and just managed to cling to the cage ahead. He hugged it between his forepaws and flipped the lock with his tooth. Buster moved back down the line, while Spider moved forward. The steam left his eyes streaming, but he got to Moonlight in the nick of time. Her cage door swung open like all the others, but the cat was clinging to the wire, too terrified to move.

"Jump!" barked Spider.

"I can't, darling."

"You can. You have to!"

"Let me die, Spider," she cried. "I've lived my life, and what does tomorrow hold? Only the pain of lost love—"

Her last words turned into a gasp, for Spider had her round the neck. He dragged her out, hoping he might throw her to safety, but alas, it was too late for that. They were directly above the vat, and a foul, glutinous liquid bubbled and spat, the froth splashing their paws.

Moonlight yowled in terror, as Spider lost his footing and fell. Somehow he managed to grip the rim of the vessel with his fore-paws, and somehow he twisted himself back over the edge. He writhed, and spat Moonlight on to the ground, launching himself after her. They rolled together on the hard concrete floor.

Alarms were ringing now, as animals dived for cover; the factory workers gazed in helpless wonder.

Buster appeared, and butted Spider into action again. There was no time to lose, for an enormous grille was descending, blocking their escape.

"Stay together!" snarled the pit bull. "Follow me!"

She dived into a nearby chute, and the whole pack rushed after her, a heaving mass of ears and tails. They found themselves slithering downwards on their backs to land with a clattering crash among empty tins. Spider lay entangled with the lurcher, while a skinny dachshund he'd never seen before wormed its way, yapping, from under his rump. They were on another conveyor belt.

"What now?" cried Moonlight as they sailed onwards.

"I don't know," Buster panted. "Hold tight, I guess! It's not over yet, guys..."

They were in the bowels of the factory, where steel levers gathered the tins into organized lines. A set of pipes appeared over their heads, and a dark substance dripped from a dozen nozzles in stinking lumps. A welding mechanism flashed as it sealed those that were full. Spider took the initiative this time, and as he came under the first nozzle he threw himself sideways into a tunnel that bent sharply to the left. The animals plunged after him, skimming helplessly into a mountain of soft powder. When they'd managed to clamber free, every creature was snow white from nose to tail.

"Flour," said the flea in Spider's ear. "Keep moving."

"We're still alive!" cried Buster. "Let's keep it that way, guys. We're doing well."

"Which way is out?" asked Moonlight. "I need daylight."

Spider shook himself and saw a door.

"That way!" he cried. "Move it!"

The door gave out on to a corridor, and he stood back as the line of animals dashed past him. Seconds later, they were in a warehouse. A forklift truck buzzed between storage racks, its light winking. Buster led the way again, dashing down the aisles in search of an exit.

They were soon lost and bewildered, for every shelf was solid with identical cartons. The picture Spider had seen by the bins was reproduced ten thousand times: the same smiling woman served a glutinous gunk to the same eager pets. As the animals stared, mesmerized, a guard appeared. Two more stepped into the space behind them, and they saw they were trapped.

The lurcher started to bark, and there was soon an ominous howling as the pack squeezed together. Every dog and cat prepared its claws, ready for the fight. The guards, meanwhile, were calling for back-up.

"We'll have to break through," panted Buster. "We need a fire exit. If we could find one of them, it might save us."

"A fire alarm," said the flea.

"What about it?"

"That would buy us time. Panic and confusion are what we need, so let me on to that stack, Spider. Above your head."

"Why?" whined Spider. "We don't have time! They're coming for us."

"Stand still," cried the flea. "It's an old trick, but it never fails…"

The animals watched as the tiny insect hopped from Spider's ear to the nearest shelf. It leapt again, vaulting up the cartons towards a thin wire. For a moment they lost it, but—even as the guards advanced—it reappeared beside a bright red box. It squeezed through the seal, and seconds later, Spider saw a tiny spark.

The building erupted in howling noise. Sirens wailed, and a metallic voice burst from overhead speakers: "Emergency! Emergency!"

The words were repeated over and over, and the guards had no choice but to run for it.

The flea pushed its way back out of the box, dazed and unsteady. It dived, and Spider caught the exhausted insect right on his nose. It was hot as a cinder.

"Go," it cried weakly. "I short-circuited the system, but it won't give us long."

"Wait," hissed Moonlight. "Look at the roof, Spider. That's a cooling system up there, I'm sure of it. If we could get inside, we'd find our way out."

"You mean climb?" said Buster. "How?"

"I don't know," Moonlight replied. "I don't have the strength, but the rest of you might make it."

The animals gazed up at the warehouse roof. Sure enough, there were ducts and pipes above their heads, and the fattest was almost within reach.

"It's our only chance," said Spider. "What we need is a ladder."

"Behind you," said a terrier.

A pair of ragged spaniels raced down the aisle to a set of steps. They grabbed its rail between them and it was soon in position. The next moment, Moonlight had jumped nimbly up its rungs, and was soon close to the vent. Spider struggled after her.

"There's a bracket," he barked. "Get on to that, and you can open the hatch."

"I know what you're looking at!" she cried, as she wrapped herself round the pipe. "You're laughing at my tail!"

"Just go!" barked Spider. "Hurry…"

"They'll be back," growled Buster. "We have to keep moving!"

Moonlight snapped the flap open with her paw, and the animals scrambled into the gap as best they could. They used their jaws and their paws, and somehow tipped themselves into the vent, hauling each other upwards. Thankfully, the chute levelled almost at once, and they were soon in a line again, trotting briskly into the gloom. When they came to an intersection, it was a Labrador that guided them.

"Fresh air," she whimpered. "I can smell it, I know I can..."

She turned right, and they all caught the scent together. They galloped now, their paws drumming on the metal, and reached a set of pumps and valves. When they'd clambered past them, they found themselves gazing upwards, for they had come to a chimney and, at last, they could see a disc of pure blue sky. The cats found the final ascent simple, but the dogs had to inch carefully upwards, bracing their backs against the metal. When they got their chins over the rim, it wasn't so hard, and they rolled over and dropped down on to the factory roof. They staggered to its edge and dropped again, into a car park. The perimeter fence proved no obstacle: they all pushed under it into a field of long, lush grass. As the alarms faded behind them, they realized they were free.

They flopped down in the sunshine, and lay dazed and aching, unable to believe their good luck. They were on a gentle slope, and a valley spread before them, so green and lovely nobody could speak. They lay there, panting, gazing at the sheer beauty of the world.

"What now?" said Buster.

"We rest," replied Moonlight. "We curl up together and lick our wounds."

"We need something to eat," said the lurcher. "We're all starving."

Most of the other animals were nodding. Some had stretched out, exhausted, and one or two had fallen asleep. The dachshund was on its back, paws in the air.

Spider, however, was silent and alert.

He had never been as thirsty or sore, and he hadn't drunk water for days. Somehow, though, he could feel his strength returning—and with it came that terrible restlessness. He couldn't stay still.

Buster padded close and butted him.

"You did well, pal," she said. "You're quick-thinking for a pet."

Spider shivered, and flipped his ears back.

"It won't go away, Buster," he said. "It's worse now. Worse than ever."

"What is?"

"The need to be found. I can't rest, you see—I need to be moving."

The flea pinched him gently. "You're getting hot again," it said. "What are you thinking now? What do you want?"

Spider lowered his head and lifted it again.

"I'm sorry," he sighed. "I just want to go on. I can't stay with you guys—you know I can't."

"Darling, wait," said Moonlight. "This is a good place. We'll find a stream and have a wash, and—"

"You don't understand," said Spider. "I don't care about washing. I don't care about food. I'm just as lost as I was, and a lost dog cannot find peace. Ever."

He walked forward, wincing at the pain in his pads.

Buster nodded and growled.

"I feel the same," she said quietly. "That's something we have in common, buddy. We're both being looked for by people that care. Why? Because we're needed. We're both loved, I guess. Remind me: what's the name of your master? "

"Tom," said Spider, and once again the word was like a bolt of electricity. He closed his eyes, and the fur on his back rose up.

"My man's called Spike," said Buster. "It's the only word I can spell—it's tattooed across his knuckles. Both hands!" The pit bull shook her head. "He'll be going crazy without me."

"Tom came out to that village," replied Spider. "He must have done, Buster. He pinned that poster to the lamp post, because he's trying to find me. So it's even more urgent now: I have to get home. And I'm sorry—because I know it's selfish—but this really is goodbye."

"Don't say that," whispered Moonlight, but the dog was staring ahead.

In the distance, a train made its way through the valley, and Spider thought of the long trek ahead. He flexed his left paw and then his right. He would find water at some point. All he knew was that he had to start at once.

"You're not going alone," said Buster.

"No," said the flea. "I'm not leaving you. I'm in this for the duration."

"Oh, please!" cried Spider. "You mustn't follow me. I'll get lost again—I'm bound to—and it could take a lifetime!"

"Stop arguing, pal," said the pit bull. "We're a team now, and that's all there is to it. We'll find your boy, and when you're safely back home together, I'll find my boss. Who's looking for you, cat?"

"Nobody."

"Really?"

"I'm free, darling. Free as a bird."

"I'm sorry to hear that."

Moonlight put her cheek against Spider's and nipped his ear. The other animals looked on in respectful silence.

"You know, Spider," she said, "I shouldn't have come between you and that little boy. You want to find him, and I understand that now. He's probably forgotten you, because boys are heartless creatures, but—"

"He's hunting for me, Moonlight. I just told you."

"Ah, you're so loyal. You always will be, with a heart like yours. We're the same, aren't we? Mad, emotional things, guided always by love."

Spider closed his eyes and swallowed. "I'm not sure we're the same, you and me," he said. "All I know is that Tom needs me, more than ever. The last time I saw him he was hurt, and he's still hurting. I abandoned him, and... something's very wrong."

"Is he in danger?" asked Buster. "Is that what you're saying?"

"Yes. I think he is."

Even as he said it, the sun disappeared behind a cloud, and he felt cold all over. He had never before felt such a strong premonition of impending doom, and he found his tail was trembling.

"Lead on," said Buster. "Are you with us, cat? You've come this far, so you'd better make your mind up."

Moonlight shook her head, then—suddenly—nodded it.

"Yes," she said quietly. "I think I should."

Just then they heard the sound of a motor. Somewhere in the distance, a moped was puttering along a lane. They heard it stop and start again, and a tiny yellow crash helmet came briefly into view before it disappeared into the far-off trees. The noise of the engine died, and was replaced by birdsong.

3

Tom was having the time of his life.

The gears on the moped changed automatically, and though he'd told himself to go carefully, he was soon bowling along happily as the wind whipped through his clothes. The fuel tank was full, and so far nobody had flagged him down to accuse him of being the selfish thief he knew he'd become. Nobody had even glanced at him.

He had ridden round the neighbouring streets first, just to build his confidence. Then he got down to his actual mission: following the main road out of town, all the way to Tayler's house. He would check every centimetre of tarmac, and prove the boy a liar. Then he would find his beloved dog.

He passed the railway station, then his school. He waved two fingers at the gates, and sailed on round the back of the church to a large roundabout. It was still swirling with rush-hour traffic, and he was unsettled by the impatience of the cars and trucks that surrounded him. They pushed past and roared into a river of fumes and metal. A break came at last, and he eased himself into it. Half a minute later he was on a slip road, which launched him on to the dual carriageway.

He accelerated hard, but found that even when his motor was screaming—and the dial said thirty-two miles an hour—he was painfully slow compared to everything else. He tried to tuck himself into the left, but there were so many drain covers and bits of old tyre that he was forced to pull out towards the centre of his lane. Vehicles surged past him, and sometimes he had to wrestle with the steering just to keep straight. A particularly huge lorry came by, and he felt his machine veering forward, wobbling into its slipstream. "McKinley's" was emblazoned on its rear, over two cartoon puppies that eagerly devoured a bowl of rich, tender meat. The picture urged him on, as the car behind blasted its horn.

After forty-five minutes, he did the return journey. He passed the sad remains of a badger and a pheasant, but there were absolutely no dead dogs. Tom started to laugh: if he ever saw Tayler again, he would have his revenge. If it came to a fight, Tom suddenly knew who'd win, and realized that he'd been timid for too long—he'd been feeling sorry for himself, and it was now time to take control.

His confidence soared, and he set off with renewed energy to scour the countryside.

Meanwhile, Spider, Buster and Moonlight had cut across the fields and come to the railway line. The flea was on Spider's nose.

They had said sad farewells to the other animals, and a brisk trot had brought them to two sets of tracks.

A whistle sounded in the distance, and Moonlight put her paw on the nearest rail.

"Something's coming," she said.

"Then we ought to stand well back," said Buster. "A pal of mine had a fight with a train, and it didn't end too well. I say we let it pass and follow."

"Why don't we just catch it?" asked the flea.

"How?" asked the pit bull.

"This is an uphill section, so the train might be going slowly. If you guys run fast, we could jump aboard."

Spider nodded. "That's a good idea. If it's going to the town, we get there faster. If we're going the wrong way, we'll just stay hidden and it'll take us back."

"Clever," said Moonlight.

Buster got to her feet. "Here she comes," she said. "Just watch out for the wheels…"

The train laboured into view, belching diesel. The tracks hummed under its weight and there was an ominous clattering. It was a long freight train, and that meant a seemingly endless line of low wagons, each carrying a square container. They trundled by, one after the other, and the animals scampered beside them. They could hardly believe their luck: the very last section was a flat wooden deck, perfect for a soft landing.

Buster jumped first, and though she stumbled, she steadied herself and sat down safely. Moonlight and Spider followed, and anchored themselves against her chest. Minutes later, they were skimming along with the wind in their fur.

"Our luck's changing," said the flea softly. "I feel confident."

"I've been lucky all my life," said Spider. "I just didn't see it."

"So we're looking for the school again, yes?"

"That's my plan. We'll just walk those streets and keep our eyes open."

He shivered again.

"What?" asked Moonlight. "Are you sick?"

"I'm hot," said Spider. "I'm thinking about Tom, and I can almost see him. He'll be in a classroom right now, with all his friends. He doesn't know I'm on his trail."

"You're getting closer all the time," said Buster, butting him gently.

"What's that ahead? I can see flashing lights."

"We're slowing down," said Moonlight.

Buster growled and walked to the edge of the wagon. The train lurched and whistled.

"You're right," she said. "It's a level crossing, and there's that motorbike again."

Spider stood up.

He was shivering violently now, and his hackles were up. His paws were itching, too, and he didn't know why.

The barriers were coming closer, and he could see several vehicles waiting to pass. Sure enough, the moped they had noticed was at the front, and its rider was staring straight at Spider, open-mouthed. As the dog drew level, their eyes met and locked together.

"This is going to sound silly," whimpered Spider, as he sailed past. "In fact, it's going to sound crazy, but that man back there... that boy on the bike..."

"What about him?" asked Buster. "Sit down, pal—you're going to fall over."

"I don't think I can. I'm trying, but I can't."

Spider trotted to the very edge of the wagon and gazed at the receding figure. It was definitely a boy, and when the barriers came up, he threw the bike to the ground, and walked right on to the tracks. He stood between the rails, absolutely still—and as he pulled off his helmet, Spider felt a curious jolt in his heart. He tried to bark, but all that emerged was a strangled croak.

"Darling," said Moonlight, "I swear you've caught a chill. When I get you home—"

"I don't believe it," whispered Spider, ignoring the cat. "Buster, you're going to think I'm making this up, but look at him now. Look..."

The dog found his voice at last, and started to howl.

"What is it?" barked Buster. "Hush now! What's wrong? Talk to me!"

"I don't know," cried Spider. "I don't know!"

"OK, keep calm. Trust your instincts, pal—that's what they're for."

"But it couldn't be," moaned Spider. He howled again and twisted round in a circle. "It *couldn't* be him, could it? The bike belongs to Phil, so Tom wouldn't be using it."

"I'm not following this at all," said the flea. "You said Tom's at school today."

"He is! Or he should be..."

At last, Spider sat down, but he was still shaking.

"I'm seeing things," he said. "Maybe I'm having hallucinations—I do need to eat—but that boy looked just like my master. Same eyes, same nose, same everything. I'm going mad..."

*

Tom was also gazing into the distance in total disbelief.

He'd ridden through several villages, combing their streets. He had continued out to the pet-food factory, and he'd sat by its gates wondering what to do next. His fuel tank was low, so he needed a garage. The problem was obvious, though: he could hardly expect his dog to materialize from thin air and leap on to the road. How could he conduct a careful, thorough search?

He had to keep going, so he opened the throttle and zipped down a quiet country lane. When he came to the level crossing, the lights had just started to flash. He accelerated hard, but the barriers were coming down as he got to them, and he had to stamp on his brake.

A bright blue sports car was waiting on the other side of the line, and its driver heard the screech of tyres. The roof was down, and the man peered at him with disapproval. Tom saw him whisper something to his passenger, who produced a tiny pair of binoculars, the sunlight flashing on the lenses. As the freight train rumbled past, Tom was glad of its length: it meant he was invisible, and he wondered about turning round and riding off the way he'd come. He was still undecided as the last wagon trundled into view.

That's when he saw three creatures in the middle of the train: a cat, a mutilated pit bull, and—like a vision—a black and white puppy with too-long legs and floppy ears. They sailed by like statues, and as he watched, the black and white dog came to life and walked to the very edge, gazing into his eyes.

Tom knew the look, and he knew the walk. He knew the tail as it gave a single, hesitant wag. He knew the gentle tilt of the head, which revealed that special tooth. It was the dog he'd missed so much, and to see him rolling past left him short of breath. The terrible thing was that he knew it was impossible, which meant he was having visions borne of sheer desperation. He watched the mirage as it shrank to almost nothing. Then he clambered off the bike as the barriers rose and ran on to the tracks.

The dog was howling. Tom yanked off his helmet and gazed: there was a volley of sharp, desolate barks as the train slipped away. The dog was still in view – and was its tail wagging harder? Was that one last, distant cry?

The boy's legs were jelly, and there were tears in his eyes. His vision was blurred, and as the train gathered speed the animal became a mere speck, getting smaller every second.

"Oh, please," he said softly.

Tom was brought back to reality by a soft toot. A Mini was inching round him, with a bemused-looking driver at the wheel. He stepped out of its way and ran back to his bike. As he did so, he heard a male voice, sharp and serious, and he knew he was in trouble. The sports car was blocking his path, and the couple inside were glaring at him.

"Excuse me, young man," said the driver. "How old are you?"

"I'd say twelve at the most," hissed the woman next to him. "He's a schoolboy, Guy. Whose bike is that?"

"I don't think it's yours, is it?" said the man. "Call the police, Helen."

"I'm twenty-one," said Tom.

"Oh, really?" said the woman nastily. "What year were you born?"

"I'm… not sure. Ages ago."

"You came down that hill like a maniac," said the man. He was opening his door. "You're from the estate, aren't you?"

"He won't be insured," hissed his wife. "Where's the pen, dear? I'll get the licence number."

Tom hauled the moped back on to its wheels, but it was far heavier than he'd expected, and he had the helmet on his arm.

The driver was following him.

"No you don't!" he said loudly. "It's other road users I'm thinking of, so give me those keys."

"Guy, be careful. He could have a knife."

"Don't ignore me!" cried the driver. "Do as you're told!"

The bike's engine was still running. Tom could hear it chugging away and knew he had half a second at the most to make up his mind. He discarded the helmet and leapt astride the saddle, opening the throttle just as the man lunged for him. He forced the handlebars round, and the machine rose up on its rear wheel before careering forward. He crashed down on to the train tracks, accelerating even harder as he bounced over the sleepers.

The couple were left gawping in astonishment, for Tom was off down the railway line itself, in pursuit of the disappearing train. He could hardly see it any more, but it hadn't been going fast. Surely he could catch it? He was doing forty-one kilometres, forty-two...

He cleared the summit of a hill and the train track sloped downwards. His speed rose to fifty and he could hear a drum roll as his tyres raced between the rails. His hair was flying, and the wind was cold in his eyes. In the distance—yes!—he could see the last wagon still, and he knew beyond all doubt that the dog on board was Spider. He also knew that all misunderstandings could be put right if only he could reach him.

He clung to the machine, shouting Spider's name. The freight train was veering slowly to the right, and it was slowing down just as he was speeding up—in another minute he would catch it.

What Tom didn't realize was that the train he was chasing was moving on to a branch line. The points had changed, and it was making way for a delayed express, which blasted its horn as the last wagon rolled clear. The signal was green and its driver pushed his speed to maximum, determined to make up some time. He came thundering through, hooting again, long and shrill—and that's when he saw Tom.

It didn't seem real.

The boy was riding a moped straight into his buffers. He wasn't even wearing a helmet, and his mouth was wide open in a mixture of horror and wonder. They both hit their brakes, and the driver closed his eyes as he waited for the crunch of metal. He would derail, he was sure of it, for the bike would go under his wheels and jerk the engine off the tracks—the poor rider would be spread over his windscreen, or chopped to pieces! He leant on the brake, praying, and when he finally dared to look up he saw only empty space.

The boy had disappeared.

Tom had acted on instinct.

The little moped was locked between the lines, so he couldn't swerve. He glimpsed the poor driver's face and heard a brain-shredding screech as the train wheels slid along the rails. There was a burst of sparks, and that's what made him haul at the handlebars, wrenching them upwards. The bike jumped, and with half a second to spare Tom wrestled it to the side and found himself landing in a spray of gravel. The front tyre exploded, and the rear fishtailed wildly as he hurtled down a footpath. Trees flashed past on either side, and he hit a root so hard that he was flipped in a long, slow somersault— the sky was underneath him, and the ground was spinning above.

He landed flat on his back in a thick bed of ferns, and lay there knowing he'd been killed. All he could hear was birdsong. Dazed, he tried to move his fingers, and was astonished to find that they did just what they were told. He could flex his toes, too, so he clearly wasn't paralysed—and nothing appeared to be broken, or even grazed. He rolled gingerly on to his side, and found that the foliage tipped him neatly back on to his feet.

He looked for the moped. It was in pieces, of course—he could see that at once. The front forks had slammed into a large conifer, and both wheels had been torn off. He gazed at what was left and thought of Phil. He thought of his dad, too, wondering what on earth he'd say. This was not the time for reflection, though: he had to keep moving.

The railway line was close, so he tottered back to it. Fifty metres down the track stood a tiny station, so he headed towards the platform and climbed the ramp. An old man was sitting on its one concrete bench, and he nodded at Tom. Then he sighed and made a mark in his notebook.

"Late again," he said.

"Am I?" asked Tom.

"What?"

"Late."

"Who?"

"Me."

"No. Not you, son. I mean the 15.06. It's on its way, but it's… seven minutes behind schedule. It was late leaving, as usual." The man chuckled.

"They won't hit their target."

"I suppose not."

Tom licked his lips, aware that his voice was cracking. His heart was pounding, too—it just wouldn't slow down.

"What's the matter?" asked the man.

"Nothing," said Tom. "I'm just a bit confused. Did you by any chance notice a big, long freight train? It would have come through here a few minutes ago. Did you see it?"

"Of course."

"It was real, then?"

"Real?"

"I'm not dead, am I? I'm definitely alive, talking to you?"

"Of course you're alive," said the man. "You're asking about the 15.11 wagon service. The locomotive's one of six, if you want the details: a Schlossenburg 35, made in Germany. She was off to the docks."

"The docks? Outside town, you mean?"

"By the old warehouses. Are you a spotter, too?"

"Yes. I suppose I am."

"I'll tell you a trade secret, then. The freight trains still get priority on this line, and that's what's behind all the disruption. What annoys me is that half those containers are empty."

Tom noticed that his legs were still shaking, so he joined the man on the bench.

"Did you by any chance see a dog?"

"Where?"

"Standing on the last wagon. He's black and white. Quite young."

"I was looking at the chassis, I'm afraid. That's the old seventies model—thirty tonne maximum, which is why they're slow."

"He's only a puppy."

"What is?"

"My dog. There was a dog on the last wagon of that freight train. I saw him, I'm sure of it."

"I doubt it, son. You don't tend to get dogs riding on trains, because of health and safety."

"You must have missed him."

The man frowned. "Possibly," he said. "I was actually cross-referencing my timetables."

He turned to the back of his notebook, hooked off his glasses and put his nose close to the page.

"Depot departure at 09.43, picking up at McKinley's. Then it goes to the cement factory. Terminates at sidings seven, where the wagons divide. The front half goes on to the pier. The back half waits at the disused warehouse, then goes out to the quarry."

Tom stood up.

"Where would it be now?" he asked. "The last wagon, I mean. Where was it going?"

"I just told you," said the man. "The warehouses. I had a little snoop around there last month, as a matter of fact—they're pulling them down, but I got some cracking photos. I'd catch this fellow here, if you want to go there. This is the delayed 15.08. Get down at the terminus."

The old man was on his feet now, for a passenger train was approaching.

"Darren!" he cried, as the driver's cab drew level. "You're three minutes late. Any excuse?"

"Not really," replied the driver. "Bit slow at the crossing—there's a police car down there, looking for some hooligan. Stole a motorbike, apparently, and threatened a couple of pensioners. He had a knife, too—gave them quite a mouthful."

Tom said nothing.

He climbed quietly on to the train and took a seat. Taking off his coat, he discovered that he was still wearing his school blazer, with its thin red stripe. His tie was in his pocket, so he put it on. His hands were filthy, and his shoes were scuffed. He had leaves in his hair, and his trousers were thick with mud. In fact, he looked like a perfectly normal schoolboy, and his fellow passengers hadn't even glanced at him.

A bell rang, and the doors closed. The train shunted forward, and Tom was on his way again.

Twenty minutes later, he saw the familiar rooftops of his own town, dominated by the church tower.

He had his route worked out and was ready to run. He was first through the doors, and hardly noticed the clusters of children waiting to board. He didn't see Robert Tayler—he simply pushed through the scrum and set off at a sprint.

Rob nudged his companion and stared.

"That was Lipman," he said. "Where's he going?"

The friend smiled. "Where's he been? That's the question. He wasn't at school today, so why's he in his uniform?"

"He's bunking off."

"He's scared, by the look of it. Why's he going that way?"

They watched as Tom reached the end of the platform and jumped down on to the tracks.

"Shall we follow him?" said Robert. "He's on his own, as usual—we could sort him out properly. Once and for all…"

5

Tom stepped carefully. The lines were a confusing tangle, but he walked along the sleepers as quickly as he dared. Any minute, he'd be spotted and someone would raise the alarm—he knew he was trespassing, and he knew he was taking a suicidal risk. One slip, and he'd be roasted: he'd been told that if you touched a live rail, your flesh would stick to it, sizzling. To give up now, though, was unthinkable. Spider had to be close.

The line he was following divided, and at last he saw a freight train.

Was it the right one? It was some way off, and had come to rest between two derelict platforms. The low wagon at the end was flat and bare, and he had the sense that he'd been hallucinating again, for it looked as if the train had never moved. It might have been sitting for ever in its own little wasteland. Wild grass grew high, and there was an ominous silence, as if all the birds had taken flight. He reached the wagon and clambered up on to it. There were warehouses further along, and "Keep Out" notices had been screwed to a long, collapsing fence. Razor wire glinted in the sunshine, but there were holes everywhere—a dog could easily get through. Tom knew he had to keep going.

He dropped to his knees and found a gap the width of his shoulders. Half a minute later, he had squirmed his way on to a building site. A bulldozer sat quietly, without a driver. Beyond it stood the structure it had been demolishing: a huge carcass of cracked walls and empty windows and a caved-in roof. There was a crane with a wrecking ball—that too was still and lifeless.

Tom whistled, but it wasn't the kind of whistle that carried.

"Spider!" he cried—and he realized how long it had been since he'd shouted the name.

He called again, at the very top of his voice, "Come on, boy! Spider?"

Spider turned, and found his tail was wagging. He'd jumped off the wagon long before it had reached the warehouse, for what he wanted was the railway station. Moonlight had led the way, and they had reached it minutes before Tom's train arrived. This time, the platform was full of red and black blazers, and Spider barked in delight. They were worn by genuine schoolchildren, and the golden lions were clear to see. Buster and Moonlight hung back anxiously as Spider ran among them, skipping from group to group like a sheepdog. He pushed his way through, revisiting certain clusters in dismayed disbelief: Tom simply wasn't there.

He scampered back to his friends, for he was attracting far too much attention. Buster felt his frustration, but pushed him back into a quiet corner.

"Calm yourself down," she said. "We're closer than ever—we must be."

"I don't know," whimpered Spider. "Was that really him on the motorbike? If it was, then he wasn't at school."

"How could it have been?" said the flea. "Let's keep to the side—everyone's looking at us."

"You know, darling," said Moonlight. "I've had an idea. Why don't we just go back home and wait for him there? He's bound to turn up sooner or later, and we might even get some dinner."

Spider barked in frustration.

"How can I?" he cried.

"Cat," snarled Buster, "he doesn't know where home is. That's why we're looking for the wretched school!"

"But it's just round the corner," said Moonlight.

"Where?" Spider asked. "What do you mean?"

The cat sat down and licked her paw. "Your little house. The place we met, when you followed me on to the roof and opened your heart. It's close to the park, isn't it?"

Spider nodded. "Yes, very close."

"It's five minutes from here, angel. Do you want me to show you?"

"Moonlight," said Buster, "are you serious?"

The cat blinked. "Of course," she said. "I should have thought of it before, really."

Spider moved in front of her and put his nose close to hers.

He was panting. "Don't play games," he said. "Are you telling me that you could lead me home to Tom? Is that what you're saying?"

The cat's eyes were wide. "Why, yes," she said.

"You're positive?"

"Of course."

"Then why didn't you say so ages ago?" cried the flea.

"Nobody asked. You were talking about getting to the station, so I thought you had a plan."

"Moonbeam, you're a menace!" roared Buster, snarling furiously.

"We're looking for this dog's owner, yes?"

"Little Tom, of course—"

"So get that stump of a tail in gear! Get your skinny arse moving and get this dog home. Now!"

The pit bull snapped at Moonlight's bottom, and she leapt into the air, yowling. She cringed as the pit bull glared, but managed to turn primly and put her nose in the air. Seconds later, she was trotting across the station concourse towards the exit, and the others were right behind her.

Five minutes after that, Spider recognized his first landmark: a pair of iron gates stood wide open, revealing an expanse of green grass. They entered the park together and sprinted to the far side. Spider now knew exactly where he was, and identical gates let him out across a road. He was soon in a labyrinth of alleyways, and he could have negotiated them with his eyes closed. He was leading now, though Moonlight was next to him. He was whining, too, unable to help himself, for he could smell rich, familiar smells. Suddenly he was passing the first door on his very own street! The white door was next to it, and they reached the house that smelt of spices, which joined on to the boarded-up shop. And there it was, at last: the home he'd so stupidly abandoned. He looked up at its peeling yellow paintwork, and his heart jolted painfully. He'd caught his first scent of Tom.

Above his head was a poster, pinned above the knocker, and Spider saw himself in the arms of his master.

"Oh," Spider said, trembling again. "Buster, look!"

"There it is," said the pit bull. "He wants you back, pal—you were dead right. He'll be in there now, waiting for you. You've made it."

Spider's mouth was dry. He was feeling faint, so he sat down in front of the door and scratched at the wood. Within seconds, he was up again, with his nose through the letter box, barking loudly.

Buster joined him, and Moonlight jumped on to the front room's window sill to stare through the glass.

Nobody answered.

"Stop," said the flea. "You'll get us arrested."

"He must be in there," cried Spider. "School's finished—we saw that."

He yelped twice, but this time he was aware of the unsettling quiet. His cries echoed in the empty hallway and were swallowed by silence.

"Is there any other way in?" asked the flea.

Spider swallowed. "Only one," he said. "The skylight."

"I'll go," said the cat. "It's quite a climb, but I'll do my best. Wish me luck, darling, and wait for me…"

Tom picked his way over the rubble towards what was left of
the warehouse. It was old brick, and as he passed through its
gaping doors he could see how precarious the structure was.
Sections of the upper floors had given way, and he could see
right up to a skeleton of steel girders and rotting timbers.
The sky was visible beyond, while under his feet the floor was
cobbled, and he was surrounded by crooked pillars and posts.
There were several staircases, but most led only to empty
space; others took you up to crumbling galleries. The sun fell
in hard, diagonal shafts, and he had the strangest feeling that
he was being watched.

Why would Spider be *here*? Tom was about to turn and

continue the search elsewhere, when he heard a stone rattle on one of the upper floors.

He shouted again, "Spider!"

This time his voice echoed back at him and faded to nothing. A pigeon took flight, dislodging a trickle of dirt. There was a high-pitched yelp from behind, but when he swung round there was only stillness.

"Come on, boy," he said quietly. "What's wrong, Spider? Where are you?"

He chose the one set of steps that looked reasonably sturdy and started to climb.

Robert Tayler, meanwhile, was struggling not to laugh.

He'd followed Tom through the fence, having been behind Tom for some time, astonished he hadn't been seen. He turned round, grinning. Marcus was still with him, and the plan was working beautifully. The boys realized they could go slowly now. They put their bags and blazers on the ground, and as Tom disappeared into the warehouse they tiptoed round it. Sneaking through the side, they watched as Tom gazed upwards. It was Marcus who threw the stone. When Tom started to climb, they chose a staircase opposite, and minutes later they were above their victim, looking down. When Tom appeared, they crouched low.

Robert lobbed a roof tile this time, aiming high. It dropped hard on to a metal girder and there was a violent clanging. Marcus answered it with a volley of realistic barks, and they had the satisfaction of watching Tom spin round in panic.

"Spider!" he cried. "Where are you, boy? I'm not angry."

Robert yelped.

"Spider? Please..."

The impression of a dog in pain was perfect, and the echo made it all the more plaintive. Tom was beside himself.

He cried out again, "Spider!"

Then he moved quickly upwards, and found himself on a wooden deck, way up in what was left of the attic.

That was when Robert noticed a thin, metal rod. It was lying close to his feet, straight as a poker, and it was the ideal implement of terror. He picked it up and cut off Tom's exit.

"Got you," Robert said.

Tom looked down, and the two boys stared at each other.

"Your dog's dead, Lipman. So are you."

Back at the house, Thread the spider could not believe its eyes. Its skylight was opening from the outside, and it could see a skinny grey paw pushing at the glass.

"Hey, back off!" it cried. "What's going on?"

"I'm looking for a boy," said Moonlight. "A little boy called Tom. This is his bedroom, isn't it?"

"Tom who? Get back! This is private property."

"This is also his room—I know it is. Is he here or not?"

"No. He's run away."

"Don't say that!" cried the cat. "Spider's arrived. He's come all this way to see him."

She forced her head inside and found herself staring down at an empty, unmade bed. In a moment, she had squeezed under the window and dropped to the wardrobe. Ignoring the spider's cries, she jumped to the floor. The bedroom door was open so she padded through nervously. By the time she got downstairs, it was obvious that the whole house was deserted, so she leapt on to the kitchen counter—and there was Spider in the back garden, barking desperately.

Moonlight butted the casement window and flipped the catch with her paws. Seconds later, Spider had hurled himself through the opening and was inside.

"Spider, wait!" she cried, but it was no use.

The dog rolled himself past her, falling heavily on to dirty crockery. He shook the splinters from his fur. The next moment, he was racing up to the bedroom he remembered so well. The scent of Tom was everywhere, but even as he skidded to a halt and gazed around him, it was obvious that yet again he'd failed in his quest. Tom was agonizingly absent.

Thread let himself down and dangled just above his head.

"This is an outrage, Fido," he hissed. "First a mutilated cat, and now you. We all thought you were dead."

"You know who I'm looking for," panted Spider. "Where's he gone?"

"He's a fugitive, as far as I know. And, by the way, you've got a flea on your face."

"He certainly has," said the flea. "And I've been looking forward to meeting you for a very long time. Tell us what you know—and don't lie."

"Did he go to school today?" yelped Spider. "Help us, Thread—I need to find him."

The spider chuckled and twirled. "You really want the truth?" he cried. "You can have it, dog—because it's all down to you. It's been chaos round here ever since you left. The phone's been ringing non-stop, and we've even had the police round—"

"The police? Why? When did you last see Tom?"

"This morning, of course! He cried himself to sleep last night, as usual. Oh, my goodness, you wouldn't believe the tears. Then up he gets, and I'm on the landing, listening as the lodger comes upstairs. That's when your boy makes his move. He's a delinquent now, you know: he stole the motorbike and skipped school. Sometime later, two policemen showed up, talking about a road accident—"

"But where is he now?" barked Spider.

"Who knows?" shouted Thread. "We're waiting for news. They found the bike on the railway line, smashed to pieces. The rider vanished—under the train, presumably—"

"Oh, God!" howled Spider. "I don't know what to do! I can't stay here…"

He raced down the stairs, retracing his steps to the garden. Moonlight followed, and in no time they were back at the front door. Buster was on the front step, keeping guard.

"He's gone, and he's hurt," said Spider. "What do we do?"

"Eat," said Moonlight. "Let me find you something—"

"I'm not hungry, you fool! I'm never going to eat again, unless it's with Tom."

"Don't say that, Spider!"

"Why not?"

"Because you have to keep your strength up. And, oh, look— where's your flea? You've left it behind."

Moonlight went to nuzzle him, but Spider spun away from her. The next moment, he was standing motionless, a paw in the air.

"What?" asked the pit bull.

"Leave me," said Spider. "Don't touch me…"

"Why not? What's wrong?"

"It's his heart," whispered Moonlight. "It's breaking, I think—"

"Spider, talk to us!" barked the pit bull. "What's happening, pal?"

225

The dog lowered his head and swallowed. His ears started to twitch, and the fur along his backbone rose, hair by hair. He could feel the strangest tingling sensation, and the tip of his tail was hot.

"Tom is close," he said softly. "He's close, Buster—and he needs me. I can feel it."

He whined, and sniffed the air. The tingling had turned to a persistent throbbing, and he'd never felt anything as intense before. It was an awful pounding of the blood in both his heart and his head. He turned in a circle and managed to gasp.

"Why am I standing here?" asked Spider.

"You shouldn't be," said Buster. "Find him."

"Which way? I can't tell where it's coming from, but he's... he's calling me!"

"Listen harder," said Buster. "I've had this myself, buddy, so don't resist it! What can you see?"

"I see that railway again."

"What else?"

"I see... the train, the one we were on, and... we're too late."

"We can't be!" cried Moonlight.

As she spoke, they heard a siren. Somewhere nearby, an emergency vehicle was answering a call, and it jerked Spider into action. He barked once, and it was a triumphant bark, because it was the bark of realization. Suddenly, he knew which way to go. His tail was up, and in an instant he was gone—he seemed to rise upwards like a missile, and then he was flying down the pavement. Buster and Moonlight followed, but he was way ahead of them. They saw him flash across the street, as a police car missed him by a whisker.

Buster picked up his scent and gave chase. She was in time to see him coursing down an alleyway, back towards the town

226

centre. They were soon in front of the church, its familiar clock tower rising high above their heads. It was chiming five, the bells crashing over the town like an awful countdown. Spider ran yet faster, bounding into the station. He raced over the concourse to the first platform that he came to. He dodged a railwayman, who tried to block his path, and sailed over a barrier. Then they were all on the tracks, and Spider caught a whiff of his master. He forged ahead, faster than ever. A horn blasted as a train lurched slowly towards them. They scrambled under it, rolling between its wheels on to a patch of scrub. There, the lines divided, and the freight wagons came into view.

They gathered on the empty platform, but now a fence blocked their way. Spider jumped at it, barking, for he could smell his master on the stone and in the grass. The boy had been here, not long ago, and he wasn't alone.

"Help me, Buster," he whined. "We have to get through."

"This way!" cried the cat. "There's a gap just here."

"Is Tom still close?" asked the pit bull.

"Yes, but he's not safe. He's in the most terrible danger."

7

Tom felt the floorboards he was balancing on shift beneath his feet. He was aware of cracks in the brickwork, which frightened him. Another couple of roof slates slipped, and he heard them shatter below. He heard the freight train, too, blasting a long whistle as it heaved its way out of the sidings.

"Spider!" he cried. "Where are you, boy? Spider!"

"He's dead," said Robert Tayler. "How many times do you need telling?"

Tom looked down at him. "He's alive."

"Are you calling me a liar?"

"That's all you do," said Tom. "You lie all the time. You don't know what the truth is."

He looked at the metal rod the boy was holding, and realized the moment had come. His enemy was climbing towards him, smiling, and Tom felt a curious calm—there was no way to avoid the conflict any more. It had been coming for a long time, like a slow train, and there was a terrible rightness to it. They were in the perfect place: the drop was deadly, and there was no escape. An idiot might clamber on to what was left of the wall, and over the rafters, but you'd have to be mad to try. Tom's eyes flicked right and left, then focused on Rob, who was still smiling.

Marcus was behind him, looking nervous.

"You're a freak, Lipman," said Rob.

"Am I?"

"You're so scared. You're such a little weakling."

"But I'm not."

Rob waved his weapon like a sword.

"You're scared," he cried. "Just look at you."

"I'm not scared at all," replied Tom. "I'm working out how many of your bones I'm going to break. You're a rotten, wretched liar, and I'm going to batter you. I don't care about your little mate because it's you I'm after."

Rob blinked. He found that his mouth was open, and though he held the metal rod in both hands, he was no longer quite so confident. His eyes had widened, and Tom could see that he wasn't sure what to do.

"Guys," said Marcus, "this isn't safe."

"Who cares?" said Tom.

"I'm serious," Marcus said. "Let's go down and talk."

Tom took a step forward. "What shall we talk about, Tayler? You're nothing, you know. Spider's alive, and I'm going to find him. But first, I'm going to kill you."

229

Rob raised his weapon again, but now it was to defend himself. He went to speak, but before he could, Tom did a very clever thing. He'd seen it in a film, but he was amazed to find it worked so well.

He shouted, "Marcus, no!"—and that made Rob turn, giving Tom the split second he needed.

His feet were firmly planted and he let his enemy have it: a heavy right-hander that cracked into the boy's face so hard Tom felt the shock up to his shoulder. Rob was knocked off balance, utterly stunned, and Tom moved in again, grabbing at him with both hands. He had Rob's tie in his fist, up near his throat, so he yanked the boy forward and threw him sideways. Down he went, the weapon skittering into the void. Tom stepped back to use his feet: all he wanted was to kick the boy's head clean off his shoulders.

Someone had told him that you should always fight fair, but his enemy had asked for this for so long, and was now on all fours, totally at his mercy. The rage and hurt boiled in Tom, and he kicked with his right foot as hard as he'd punched. Luckily for them both, he misjudged it. The kick went wide, and Rob scrabbled to his feet, his face a mask of blood-splashed panic.

Marcus was shouting something, but Tom was ready again, thrilled that his opponent's nosebleed looked so serious.

He punched again, and caught Rob full in the mouth. The boy couldn't defend himself, and staggered back, staring into Tom's burning eyes.

He knew he was beaten, and he knew he had to run. Tom was blocking the stairs, so he took his chance, scrambling up on to the brickwork behind him. It was the only way, and he could just make it round if he jumped.

"Rob, no!" cried Marcus, but then he fell silent.

Rob had dropped to his knees, for he had misjudged it. He put his arms out, horrified to find that the parapet he was on was way too narrow. It was also sickeningly high. With nothing on either side, it was like balancing on a tightrope, and even Tom saw the terror and indecision as Rob lifted his right foot without knowing where to put it. He wanted to turn and get back to safety, but he also wanted to stay away from his attacker.

Marcus put his hand out, and Rob just managed to grab it. He jumped, and as he landed, hard, they all felt the timbers shift and tilt. A roof girder above them broke loose and smashed downwards like a hammer. A section of brickwork toppled slowly inwards and burst into a shower of rubble.

The warehouse was finally collapsing.

The boys went down with it, in an avalanche of timber, brick and slate. Everything fell in terrible slow motion, the columns and archways crumbling in upon each other.

When the debris had finally settled, a dust cloud rose up and hovered over the devastation, boiling in a soft, grey fog. Then silence reasserted itself, as if nothing of any significance had happened.

8

Spider squirmed through the fence as the last tremor died away. The stillness returned, and the site seemed deserted. Nothing moved except a curious dust cloud, which expanded slowly outwards. He could see the roof of a bulldozer buried in a pyramid of stone.

He snuffled in the grass, for once again there was the scent of something familiar—a distinctive smell of cloth. He followed the trail, and there they were: two red and black blazers, folded over two school bags. Neither belonged to Tom—he knew that at once—but he also knew he was getting closer.

Buster limped towards him on aching paws, and they gazed at one another in silence.

"Trust those instincts," said the pit bull.

"I'm trying. He's here somewhere—I know he is."

As he spoke, they heard the faintest of cries.

Both dogs leapt forward and clambered on to the debris. Spider barked a volley of short, piercing barks, but they were swallowed again by total silence.

"Be careful," whispered Moonlight.

"Why?" asked Spider.

"I smell danger, angel. It's all around us."

"I don't care. He was calling me, wasn't he? I heard his voice!"

The dog was shivering all over again. His tail was up, and the throbbing had returned. He whined and barked as loudly as he could. He threw his head back and howled. He filled his lungs again and cried like a werewolf. At once, a boy's plaintive voice found strength, and called out once more. It was weak, but the animals heard it clearly: a forlorn, exhausted cry for help.

Moonlight led the way, racing among the rubble. Tom's scent was rising from somewhere, so Spider bounded this way and that, hunting for a way down. He found a narrow gap at last. It was between two lumps of masonry, but it was scarcely wider than his head. He pushed into it, and the passage opened at once into a narrow cave. Buster joined him, and they could both see that it zigzagged into the depths like a chimney. While they hesitated, a wooden spar groaned and split, and everything shifted.

"Tom's underneath us," said Spider.

"Let me go first," said Buster. "If the way's blocked, I'll deal with it."

Without waiting for a response, the pit bull scampered forward and wormed her way into the darkness. Spider was right behind her, and Moonlight followed.

The chute turned at once into a horribly tight elbow, and they found themselves slithering. Only then did they see the true horror of the situation. They had come to a low, dimly lit chamber. A section of brickwork was tilting inwards, held up by a girder that was about to give way. A slab of concrete rested heavily on that, and there was a constant trickle of smaller stones.

"We haven't got long," Spider whispered.

"I know."

"We shouldn't be here!" said Moonlight. "We can't help him, darling. If he's down here—"

"Keep still," said Buster. "Let's think about this. Can you smell him? My nose is full of dirt."

"He's so close," said Spider. "I'm not leaving him."

"Do you think he's alive?"

"Definitely. What's that between those blocks? I can see something white."

Moonlight gasped. "It's a hand!"

"I think you're right," said the pit bull. "We're too late."

Spider launched himself and landed beside it. He hunched over the little fingers, pushing at them with his nose. He turned them and licked at the palm, nipping the thumb and willing it to move. Just as he'd given up hope, the fingers flexed. They stretched, reaching out towards the dog's mouth, and they touched his distinctive tooth. They ran over it gently, and then they reached up to stroke his muzzle. Spider pawed frantically at the rubble, and in a moment the wrist emerged, clad in a dusty sleeve of red and black. Spider yelped in joy, and gripped the fabric in his jaws. He pulled and pulled, and the arm curled right around his shoulder. Moonlight joined them, pawing the debris away, and at last they saw human hair. Spider forced his muzzle into the grit around it, twisting and lifting, and they saw a cheek, a closed eye and pale, bloodless lips. The whole face seemed lifeless, but as Spider licked it, the eyes blinked open and focused. The other arm shook itself free and, though he was weak and in pain, Tom managed to embrace his dog.

"Oh, Spider," he croaked. "At last…"

Spider couldn't stop licking the boy, and in a moment his face was clean. Buster and Moonlight were scrabbling at the masonry that crushed his legs, and Tom managed to twist himself loose. He got a leg free, and they worked together to ease the largest stone, which trapped his other knee. Tom rolled on to his front, then crouched on all fours, unable to believe he was alive. Spider whined, and Moonlight leapt towards the exit above their heads, mewing in fear.

"No," hissed Tom. "We can't leave."

Spider stared at him.

"There's two more, Spider. We can't leave them, can we? They're here somewhere. Help me dig!"

Tom plunged his hands into the rubble, and the animals realized something was still horribly wrong. Almost at once, a new scent reached their noses, and they set to work. Within minutes, they'd uncovered a shoeless foot, and an arm in a torn, white sleeve.

Tom was gasping and choking, for the dust was thickening around them.

"Marcus!" he cried. "Rob!"

The two boys were lying face down. It took another long minute to uncover them, and when they managed to raise their heads it was obvious they were nearly done for. The smaller of the two, Marcus, managed to get up on to one knee. He coughed, and Tom helped him to free his other leg. His friend was hardly conscious, and Tom moved to his side.

"Come on, Rob," he said. "You're not dying here!"

"Mum?" whispered Rob.

"It's Tom."

"Help me, Tom. I can't feel my legs."

"You have to move, OK? I can't carry you."

"Is that you, Lipman?"

"Yes!"

"I'm a liar, aren't I? I'm so, so sorry, but—"

"I don't care about that!" cried Tom. "Just get up and push, OK? Use your arms!"

Marcus was on his knees beside them and managed to grab his friend's shirt. He worked with Tom, and at last the third boy was hauled clear. They lifted Rob from behind, and Moonlight was waiting for them. She led the way up the slope towards the tiny circle of daylight above their heads. Marcus squirmed to the front, pulling at Rob behind him. Tom came last, taking some of his old enemy's weight as the bricks slid under their feet.

Another section of stone was crumbling, and it was Buster's one good eye that saved them, for she noticed the girder again, even as it shifted. She wedged her thick body against the metal, and Spider heard her gasp as it crushed her. Her lungs were straining, and she was snarling in pain. Somehow she braced herself, and the three boys scrambled past. Buster followed, just in time, and they reached the surface as the ground sucked and plunged beneath them.

They clambered backwards, to safety, as the tunnel collapsed in on itself.

Spider looked at Tom, and Tom looked at Spider.

They were covered in filth. They could hardly breathe, and their bodies were torn and bleeding. They were alive, though, and when Tom fell to the ground it was not through exhaustion or weakness—it was to embrace a true friend and hold him close.

"You're a good dog," whispered Tom through his tears. "You're the best, Spider. The best in the whole, wide world."

9

There were just three beds in the boys' ward. Marcus had the first, and Rob had the third. Tom lay between them.

They had been kept in overnight for tests, for they all had mild concussion and they'd inhaled lungfuls of dust. There seemed no end to their cuts and bruises, but amazingly, no bones were broken. They couldn't really understand why they had to stay in bed at all.

Tom's father arrived, and was ominously quiet.

When Phil joined him, nobody could speak. They sat together on Tom's bed, and the silence seemed unbreakable.

"I had to find him," said the boy, at last.

"I know," said Phil.

"I didn't know what else to do. Your bike…"

"It doesn't matter."

"Why doesn't it?" said Tom. "You should be angry with me. You should be battering me. I'm so sorry."

Phil shook his head and extended his hand. Tom's was bandaged, and he tried not to wince as Phil squeezed it firmly.

"It just doesn't matter," Phil said.

"But I said such horrible things."

"Don't we all?"

"*You* don't. I didn't mean them, Phil. You're like a brother, and… I'm sorry. And I'll pay—"

"Listen," said his father. "Listen to me for a minute, please."

The man was struggling to find the words he wanted. He looked at his son and tried again.

"I've been a fool," he said, at last. "There are things I should have said, a long time ago. There are things I shouldn't have said—and things I shouldn't have done. Things that I'm ashamed of, Tom, because I've been so… frozen up. Do you follow me?"

"Not really, Dad."

"Not at all?"

"No."

They looked at each other.

"Am I in big trouble?" asked the boy.

"Of course you're not. Not with me, not with Phil. We'll talk to the police later, but… We're going to make things so much better. They've been bad, and we're going to put them right. This is going to help us."

"How?"

"I don't know. But it will."

There was a silence again.

"Excuse me, Mr Lipman," said Rob. He'd heard the conversation, naturally, and he spoke quietly.

"What?"

"I'm sorry to interrupt, but I was the one who picked on Tom. I was... evil to him."

"We both were," said Marcus.

"I was the worst, and I don't know why," said Rob.

He was close to tears.

"Listen, please," he said. "I... I don't want to be that person any more, because I think you have the bravest son in the country—if not the world. He saved my life, and he saved Marcus, too. It's true, Mr Lipman. We're not lying."

"I know," said Tom's father.

He was pinching his nose, but if he thought Tom hadn't seen his tears, he was mistaken: one had plopped right on to the bed sheet.

"I'm truly sorry, Tom," said Rob, at last.

"I am too," said Marcus. "And we'll make it up to you."

"It's fine," said Tom.

"How can it be fine?" Rob asked.

"It is. Everyone's sorry, and that means... That means it's over."

"I'll tell you who's really brave," Marcus said. "Your dog, Lipman. Tom, I mean."

The three boys nodded.

"Not as brave as the bulldog, though," said Rob. "And the cat! Are they all yours? I didn't know you had three pets—I thought you only had one. You're so lucky—I've got a sleepy gerbil, and that's all I'm allowed. Three proper pets, and they all look after you—and each other! How amazing is that?"

Tom looked at his dad.

"Three pets," he said. "Yes, it's nice to have three."

Mr Lipman nodded. "Three's a good number, for a family."

"It always was," said Tom. "It was the best."

"I suppose the pets—they, er... keep each other company?"

"They do, Dad. Nobody gets lonely."

"And they get on?"

"Totally."

"Then we can't separate them, can we? There's been too much separation."

Tom's dad wiped his eyes and closed them. He swallowed, and Tom realized his father was nervous.

"What?" asked Tom. "What's the matter?"

"I need to tell you something," said his dad. "Your mum's outside. She sat with you all night, while you were sleeping, and she's been here all morning. We both have. She's just too scared to come in."

"Too scared?" said Tom.

"She's terrified, love. Will you speak to her?"

Tom lay back, and, for the first time in a long time, he smiled. Then, suddenly, he started to laugh. It hurt his chest and it hurt his throat, but he wasn't going to stop. He grabbed the sheet and pulled it over his head, closing his eyes as he did so. He couldn't quite face the moment, so he lay there in the darkness, waiting.

A door opened, and still he waited. At last, a pair of arms embraced him tenderly, and he let himself be held. They lifted him up and he was dragged into a hug so tight he was hurting again. It was a pain he welcomed, and he put his arms round his mother and hugged back harder still, until his laughter turned to sobs. She really had come back. She was there beside him, and she held him so tight he could feel her heartbeat.

10

Spider was unaware of these developments. He was in Tom's room, sprawled on the bed he loved. Buster was sitting on the carpet, Moonlight was on the desk, and all three were looking up at the skylight. A small spider was working its way carefully down to the floor, holding a little white package. The flea sat waiting.

Thread deposited it gently, and Spider jumped down to get a closer look.

"Stay back," cried the spider. "Mind those paws."

"Is he still alive?" Spider asked.

"Of course he is."

"Will he fly again?" asked Buster. "How long has he been up there?"

"A while, but he's doing OK. I need to tell you something, though: this is totally against my nature, and I'm still not sure about it."

"Come on," said the flea. "We've talked it through."

Thread snorted. "You did the talking," it said.

"And you agreed!"

"Under pressure. This is out of my larder, guys. This is a very big sacrifice."

"Do it," said the flea. "Be strong, and show mercy."

Thread snorted again. "You can't live on mercy, brother."

The spider pulled at the silk and started to cut. The flea hopped back to Spider's ear, and everyone watched in fascination, for it was such delicate work. A minute passed, and the strait-jacket was open: a thin moth worked his way out and rolled on to his back. He managed a weak smile of relief.

"Oh," he said. "Thank you."

He stretched his wings carefully and twitched them.

"Don't try to fly just yet," said Spider. He held out a paw. "I'll take you back to your shed. Someone's waiting for you."

"Who?"

"Your partner. He's been missing you."

The moth went slowly pink and squirmed on to his front.

"You know about us?" he asked. "How?"

"Oh, we bumped into each other," said Spider. "It was some time ago, but I visited your home."

"Good lord."

"He told me all about you. He just wants you back."

The moth nodded. "I don't know what to say. It's what kept me going, up there—thinking of him. We have short lives, obviously—but we had such plans."

He climbed slowly on to Spider's paw and settled. He flexed his shoulder muscles, and waited as the warmth returned.

"So," said Buster, at last. "What about us?"

She looked at Spider and raised an eyebrow.

"We're on your territory now... Are you comfortable with that? Because it won't be for long."

"It can be for as long as you like," said Spider.

"That's kind, but I don't want to intrude. Not on a tight family set-up. I mean, I like Tom, and I like his dad. I appreciate the hospitality, too, but I've got people of my own, and they're going to be mad as hell—old Spike must be going crazy. I've never been lost before, buddy—I told you that."

"You did."

"I've got to get home, and I've got to get fit."

"But I *want* you to stay," said Spider.

"For a few days, then," said Buster. "And thank you."

They looked at the cat.

"You too, Moonlight," said Spider. "Stay here, please. This is your home now, if you won't feel too 'owned'."

Moonlight looked away. She went to speak, but for some reason she couldn't think of anything to say, so she simply nodded and lay down.

Spider whined happily.

"Look, friends," he said. "I like sitting here, chatting away, but I ought to get moving. Tom's out of hospital today, and he'll be home soon. I want to be ready, so I'll just pop down to the shed with the moth—"

"Oh, Spider," said the flea.

"What?"

The cat blinked. "Look behind you, darling."

"Why?"

"Do what she says," said Buster. "But go slow—that moth's on your nose now."

Spider turned, and at first he couldn't believe it. He'd been so intent on his companions that he hadn't heard or smelt a thing, and his beloved master had tricked him. Tom had entered the house in silence, and he'd tiptoed up the stairs. He was with both his parents, and they'd all come quietly along the landing and pushed open the door without a squeak. Now they stood there, on the threshold: the boy at the front, with his mother just behind. She rested her hands gently on his shoulders, while Mr Lipman stood next to her. They had been there for a while, just gazing at the animals in pride, joy and wonder.

Spider felt something moving fast and hard. He stood up, and realized it was his tail. It lifted him, and for a moment he was twisting and turning so violently he fell over. His paws got tangled, and the moth launched himself into the air.

All the dog could do was yelp, and then he found he was in Tom's arms again. The boy had caught him as he jumped, and for a moment they were locked together in the centre of the room, their noses touching.

We're together, thought Spider. *We're home. I'll protect this family for ever—all of you. Just don't let me go.*

Acknowledgements

Dog emerged after a more sombre novel had withered and died. It was the antidote, and three friends got behind it at once, offering ideas and encouragement. They were Rachel Nicholson, Jane Fisher and my trusted agent, Jane Turnbull.

The notion of a pet with an identity crisis came from a little boy attending a talk I was giving in a primary school.

Tired of the story I was telling, he put up his hand and said, "I've got a dog."

"That must be nice," I replied.

"It's not," said the boy. "He wants to be a cat."

Everyone laughed, and on the train that evening I invented Spider.

The red and black school, by the way, is Portsmouth Grammar School—but it would never tolerate the kind of bullying Tom experiences, or employ anyone as foul as his history teacher. I hope no offence will be taken.

I would like to thank Sarah Odedina, of course, who has steered the book into port. My copy-editor, Madeleine Stevens, made countless suggestions, too, which proved invaluable. Mike Smith helped with detail at the proofreading stage.

Some books put up a fight, and some books go off the boil. It was a pleasure playing with *Dog*, and I hope you enjoy his company as much as I did.

THE BEGINNING WOODS
MALCOLM MCNEILL

'I loved every word and was envious of quite a few... A
modern classic. Rich, funny and terrifying'
Eoin Colfer

THE RED ABBEY CHRONICLES
MARIA TURTSCHANINOFF

1 · *Maresi*
2 · *Naondel*

'Embued with myth, wonder, and told with
a dazzling, compelling ferocity'
Kiran Millwood Hargrave, author of *The Girl of Ink and Stars*

THE LETTER FOR THE KING
TONKE DRAGT

'*The Letter for the King* will get pulses racing... Pushkin
Press deserves every praise for publishing this beautifully
translated, well-presented and captivating book'
The Times

THE SECRETS OF THE WILD WOOD
TONKE DRAGT

'Offers intrigue, action and escapism'
Sunday Times

THE SONG OF SEVEN
TONKE DRAGT

'A cracking adventure... so nail-biting you'll need to wear protective gloves'
The Times

THE MURDERER'S APE
JAKOB WEGELIUS

'A thrilling adventure. Prepare to meet the remarkable
Sally Jones; you won't soon forget her'
Publishers Weekly

THE PARENT TRAP · THE FLYING CLASSROOM · DOT AND ANTON

ERICH KÄSTNER

Illustrated by Walter Trier

'The bold line drawings by Walter Trier are the work of genius... As for the stories, if you're a fan of *Emil and the Detectives*, then you'll find these just as spirited'

Spectator

FROM THE MIXED-UP FILES OF MRS. BASIL E. FRANKWEILER

E. L. KONIGSBURG

'Delightful... I love this book... a beautifully written adventure, with endearing characters and full of dry wit, imagination and inspirational confidence'

Daily Mail

THE RECKLESS SERIES

CORNELIA FUNKE

1 · *The Petrified Flesh*
2 · *Living Shadows*
3 · *The Golden Yarn*

'A wonderful storyteller'

Sunday Times

THE WILDWITCH SERIES

LENE KAABERBØL

1 · *Wildfire*
2 · *Oblivion*
3 · *Life Stealer*
4 · *Bloodling*

'Classic fantasy adventure... Young readers will be delighted to hear that there are more adventures to come for Clara'

Lovereading

MEET AT THE ARK AT EIGHT!

ULRICH HUB

Illustrated by Jörg Mühle

'Of all the books about a penguin in a suitcase pretending to be God asking for a cheesecake, this one is absolutely, definitely my favourite'

Independent